PRIVATE LOVE

in a Public Place

Toni Kenyon

Published by:

Apeople Publishing

Copyright © 2012 Toni Kenyon

All rights reserved.

ISBN: 978-0-473-21829-4

Learn about other works by Toni Kenyon at
www.tonikenyon.com

For Kevin, Mark & Phil
who encourage me every day
to shoot for the stars

CHAPTER ONE

I felt as if I were in the presence of Christ himself, not a 21st century rock god. As the roar of the helicopter's rotors abated, the sound of the screaming thousands of fans who had gathered in the castle grounds to greet Jules reached our ears.

A surge of privilege and pride filled me as I walked beside the focus of their adoration and frenzy.

"It's amazing. I've never seen anything like it," I said. We'd arrived at plenty of gigs before, but never to one in a medieval castle by chopper.

"All right for you." Julian cast a morose look in my direction. "You don't have to get up there and perform in front of the fuckers."

We all knew he was scared. This was the worst time, those testing hours before the show. *Make-him-or-break-him* time it had been dubbed by the tight, disciple-like group who traveled with him. The time when, if he ate, he usually threw up. Or he would fuel himself on a concoction of chocolate and caffeine, only to bring that back up too, seconds before stepping on stage.

1

Though I alone witnessed the regurgitation ritual. A strange place to find myself, metaphorically holding the hand of a rock demigod while he unraveled - show after show after show.

"Mags!" Frederick's bellow across the large tent-like backstage community interrupted my thoughts. "Get Jules settled, would you?"

Settled. There was a joke. Calming a lobster before you threw it in a pot of boiling water would be an easier ask.

"Come on, Jules." I took my boss' cold and clammy hand and led him through the labyrinth of portacoms to the one with his initials on the door. The same logo adorned the chopper that had just delivered us to site.

"Mags, don't you ever get sick of spending hours with me in these fucking igloos?" Julian tore his hoodie off his head, threw his glasses on the wooden table that housed his requested supply of fruit and chocolate and scanned the room, looking for the coffee machine. "Where's my fucking mug?"

"Here." I pulled his Rosenthal cup from my knapsack. He'd fallen in love with one of the designer collections while browsing the internet one night and I'd managed to procure a supply of identical cups. A new darling would likely appear in the near future, but for now, before a gig, it wasn't worth my sanity not to have the current favorite on hand.

After pouring a cup of the steaming brew, he headed to the table and began the ritual of breaking up a king-size block of chocolate into individual squares. Starting at the center of the table, he laid each piece out in the spiraling shape of an unfurling fern frond. He'd eat his way from

2

the outside to the center, the last piece barely going down before it would come back up.

We had two hours before he was due on stage, with the dreaded back-stage meet-and-greet to get through and the usual wardrobe outburst. I thought I'd get the tantrum out of the way early.

"I've checked your kit. It's all here. You ready to get suited up?"

"Nup."

The same argument. I could never decide whether he truly hated the fuss, or if this had all become part of the elaborate sacrament he insisted on.

"Thirty minutes to meet-and-greet. You need to be dressed nicely for the fans." I tried to entice him into wardrobe.

"Where's your manners?" His incorrigible grin warmed my heart, even when he played difficult.

"Please," I said.

"Who's coming today?" Jules consumed the third piece of chocolate and sluiced it down with another mouthful of black coffee.

I fished out my schedule, carefully prepared this morning by Dan - tour manager extraordinaire - and distributed to every member of the team. "Two fourteen-year-olds from the local radio station."

He winced. "Any chance they could be bringing yummy mummies with them?"

"They have escorts, yes." Teenage girls were usually incoherent by the time they got backstage. Julian worked hard to put them at ease, but it was never a nice fifteen minutes. While he tried to make sensible conversation, they swooned and practically needed oxygen to stop from fainting.

"And the other four?"

"Twenty-three-year-old and twenty-seven-year-old."

He perked up. "Sounds promising."

"Males from the local wheelchair basketball team."

"Bugger!"

I loved teasing him. Even this wound up, his genuine good nature would shine through with the fans.

"Tell me you're saving the best for last – I'm still missing two." Jules cocked his head, an eternal look of hope pasted on his dark, even features.

"A couple of twenty-somethings Ted took a shine to at the local club last night. He thinks they might be right up your alley."

"Pay dirt!" He grinned, flashing me his perfect white teeth. "The dirty bastard hasn't shagged them already has he? You know how grubby drummers are."

"You'd best go ask him – he's three doors down on your left."

"I shall." Grabbing a handful of chocolate, Julian made for the door.

"Don't be long. You have to get dressed, remember."

"Will get the scoop and be straight back, boss." He ran a hand through his thick black hair, something he often did absentmindedly. He'd been in the room no more than three minutes and already it looked as if a small whirlwind had been through.

"Mags." Sheree had popped her head in through the doorway. "Have you got a minute?"

"Yeah, sure. Jules is liaising with Ted over his sex life."

"Oh, right." She winked. "He was lining up a couple of gorgeous models at the club last night. One lanky and blonde, and the other a stunning brunette."

"Yeah, well, since your girls are off limits."

Sheree pursed her lips. "Screwing the crew's not on, you know that. And, the last thing I need is one of my girls getting the pip with him. Where am I going to get another double-jointed dancer at ten minutes' notice who can do our routines?"

"This is true." The last thing any of us needed was Jules falling out with one of our dancers. Best if all relationships were kept platonic. It made touring bearable.

"And besides, the sexual tension's great for the act." Sheree knew the score, she kept her girls in line and I kept Jules in line.

But I had to admit I never failed to get turned on watching Jules and his girls perform.

Sheree sat down in one of the two-seater couches which stood at right angles to each other in one corner of the room. Without makeup and curled up in a snow-white track suit and pink trainers, she resembled the proverbial girl next door. In less than two hours she would emerge from the dancer's dressing room looking like a man-eater, an exotic creature dressed in thin strips of leather and lace who'd wrap herself in impossible coils around poles and stairs on the stage.

"You got a problem?" I sat down on the adjoining couch, picking at a bunch of purple grapes that sat in a second fruit bowl on the smoked glass table between the couches.

"Not really. Just a bit down, that's all." She plucked balls of non-existent lint from her tracksuit.

"You're missing Jeremy, aren't you?"

5

She shrugged. "Well, it's not a great life, touring."

"Is he putting pressure on you again to give it up?" I knew what husbands were like; I had a disgruntled one of my own at home.

She grimaced, holding two fingers a couple of centimeters apart. "Just a teeny, tiny bit."

"Wasn't it part of your vows - to love, honor and cherish, in sickness and in health, and through all kinds of strife and shit?"

"Jeremy's complaining there was nothing in the marriage contract about me being dragged all over the world for months on end, and simulating sex on stage with a gorgeous man in front of hundreds of thousands of people."

I couldn't believe her husband's idiocy. "He must have realized what your work involved. Jules was at your wedding, for crying out loud."

"I know, I know." She seemed almost in physical pain. "I don't think it worried him until after we got married. He's gotten strange about it all in the last couple of months. Constant snotty phone calls and texts. I think he wants me to just give it up and go home."

"And what do you want to do?" She was Jules' favorite dancer. He trusted her with his life – and effectively did on stage. She could do anything with him. So maybe it was understandable that a doting husband, sitting at home, could become a little neurotic.

"I love my job."

"But you love your husband."

She nodded. "I don't know what to do. How do you do it? Have a marriage and tour?"

"Heya, darlin." Before I could answer, Julian walked in

6

the door and planted a kiss on the crown of Sheree's head. "How's my number one girl?"

"I'm good, J. How about you?"

"Ace. Ted's got me a couple of scorchers sorted." Jules gave me a wink.

"I saw. At the club last night," Sheree said.

Without embarrassment, Julian pulled his hoodie and shirt over his head in one quick movement, exposing the muscles of his tight, athletic chest. His jeans went next. In just his purple jockeys, he idly flicked his fingers over the jackets and shirts that hung on a the wardrobe rack. "What's first up, Mags?"

"The usual. Black kicks, black sleeveless T with black shirt over the top and white tie."

"Right." He started assembling the clothing package that would slowly come off on stage. We always layered him carefully, taking the image from one of clean-cut young man to dirty rock god in three songs.

More coffee washed down another couple of pieces of chocolate.

"It's time for me to move. Literally." Sheree peeled herself from the couch and stretched her long limbs.

"Yeah, go get yourself warmed up." Julian's demeanor changed, taking on a more strident persona as he turned his mind to preparation for the show. "See you out the back shortly, yeah?"

Sheree popped a kiss on his cheek. "Aye, you will, boss."

"Crap!" Julian exploded as Sheree vacated the room.

"What's the problem?" It starts, I thought to myself.

"There's a bloody button missing. What's up with Wardrobe?"

I sighed. "Give it here - I'll take care of it." It was my job to take care of everything.

I caressed his back, as I would an ill child. Sometimes, some nights, it felt as if he really were a sick child. His body heaved again, convulsing in time with the music which rose to its crescendo above us. The contents of his stomach tripped past the very vocal chords the screaming throng were waiting to hear.

"Okay?" I wiped his mouth with a tissue as he disengaged from the small orange bucket.

He nodded, running the back of his hand over his lips, shaking himself off, like a dog trying to remove water from its soaking coat.

We moved together toward the spot where Jules would enter the stage. Bouncing in the wings he closed his eyes, lips murmuring in quiet prayer.

Dan touched his shoulder.

Cue music.

Lights up.

Deafening roar from the crowd and we were away.

I knew the show inside out. Touring did that to you. I decided for once to stay and watch the opening number. Usually my need to make sure the contents of the bucket I held were immediately disposed of outweighed my urge to enjoy the electric moment of Julian's first meeting with a new crowd.

I tucked the now covered container with its putrid contents in a tiny alcove at the side of the stage. I would dispose of it at the end of the night, as I'd done on more occasions than I cared to count. Tonight, I wanted to watch as the man I traveled with cast his spell over the throngs who screamed and bellowed for him.

As Jules invoked his magic.

As he strutted and stalked his way across the stage.

As the clothes came away.

A warm feeling began to creep over me. At one point between numbers he spotted me in the wings and flashed one of those cheeky smiles I'd seen him use to charm skintight jeans off rake-thin models. A jolt of pure electric delight shot through me. Then he went back to working his adoring crowd.

Lost in the thrill of seeing him for the first time as those out the front must see him, the measure of time eluded me. It seemed only minutes had passed before Julian appeared again at my side, stripping off sodden clothing, chugging mineral water from a bottle and waiting for me to dry him off. Feeling like a stable hand rubbing down a stallion after a winning run, the scent of him in my nostrils, the electrical pulse of his muscles flexing beneath me, I shuddered.

"How's it looking?" His piercing green eyes, pupils wide from the low backstage light, bored through me. "Do you think they're loving me out front."

I was loving him out back. "You appear to have them in the palm of your hand, as always."

"Maybe it's not just them I want in the palm of my hand." He shimmied himself into the dry white T-shirt I proffered, flicked the last of the mineral water from his bottle down my front and was back on his way to the stage.

Just inside the wings he turned toward me, his yelled words carrying just above the intro for his next set. "You

9

looked like you needed cooling off."

I reminded myself that he flirted incorrigibly with everyone on tour.

And that I had a wonderful husband at home waiting for this madness to end.

CHAPTER TWO

We'd assembled for our usual backstage debrief in Jules'
dressing room. "So, how did it look tonight, team?" Jules
knew it had looked good, but he still wanted us to tell him
how well he'd performed.

"Three out of ten." Dan winked at me.

"We aced it!" Frederick gave Jules a bear hug, lifting
him off his feet.

"Get off me, you oaf!" Jules' wild struggle to escape
Fred's vice-like embrace sent droplets of sweat sprinkling
over Sheree.

"God, you dickheads." She wiped herself down with
her forearm. "I practically swim with him on stage. I
could do without the shower now."

"Forgive me, my sweet maid." Jules swooped down to
one knee in front of Sheree, holding her hand to his lips
and stopping her mid-stride.

"Sweet maid, my arse." Dan dug me in the ribs with his
elbow. "The way you two cavort out there for all the
world to see, if she's a sweet maid then I must be Mother

Fucking Teresa."

"Grow up!" Sheree threw Dan a look that should have turned him to stone. Tearing her hand from Julian's grasp, she stalked out of the dressing room.

"What's the matter with her?" Dan's cocky expression vanished. Julian just looked mortified.

"Husband." I spoke the single word, knowing further elaboration would not be needed.

"She's not going to leave me, is she?" Julian looked up, stricken.

"Not unless she wants Dan to sue that tasty ass of hers from one side of the Europeon Union to the other."

Everyone turned on Ted, glaring at him.

"Could you try not to be a typically insensitive drummer for once in your life?" I could have hit him.

"Jesus," Julian sighed. "Don't let her hubby hear you talking about her like that."

"Hey, mate, I'm not the one who simulates sex with her every night in front of the punters. And he'll be an ex-husband in no time if he doesn't sort himself out. She's not going to give this up for him. He should pull his head in."

"Just cut it out." I'd had enough. "Don't you lot have some groupies to grope or something?"

"Don't feel like it." Julian deposited himself on the floor, sulking.

Dan and Ted cast a knowing glance at each other. Frederick eyeballed me, it was time to make a move. Jules' post-show high had evaporated and I just shrugged.

"I guess we'll be on our way." Frederick's attempts to direct the entourage out of the dressing room resembled herding goldfish.

The dressing room door closed and I turned my attention to Jules. "Come on, you." I tried to put on a smile and encourage Julian off his perch on the floor. "If you're not going to go out gadding you should head back to the hotel to bed."

"Don't want to!"

Frustration bubbled inside of me. The joy and elation of a great show had been poisoned and I knew I was going to pay the price. Some days I hated being tour mother.

Resigned to my fate back at the hotel with Jules, I dropped my tired body on the long-reach leather couch and picked up the TV remote. The oversized LCD screen burst into life, bathing the still pouting Julian in an eerie blue light. He looked little and demonic and afraid. Nothing like the evangelistic and inspiring angel who had graced the stage only hours earlier.

"I want National Geographic." The order issued, I surfed the channels, looking for a suitable nature documentary.

He settled on an exploration of the underwater world in the Pacific. The tropical, colorful aquatic life that appeared to swim right into the room and the slices of soothing background music had a mellowing effect. His mood began to lift and I watched the darkness seep out of his soul.

"We should go there."

"Go where?" I was equally entranced by the dance of a beautiful stingray.

"The Pacific Ocean." He jumped up, and startled me as he landed on the couch. An explosion of pent-up energy and excitement. "You know-" he gave me an embracing hug "-you, me the lads, a bit of scuba diving, lying in the sun."

"You don't know how to scuba dive - and besides, you can't swim." My protests fell on deaf ears.

"I can see it now." He was up off the couch again, pacing the expansive room. "We'll hire a huge boat."

I was almost dumbstruck. He'd been in a vegetative state on the floor only moments before.

"You don't like that idea." He scratched his head in the agitated way he did when he was thinking. "I know - a resort." His eyes were wide. "It'll be great. Sun, sand, scuba. You need to book something for after the tour."

"Get outa bed!" Dan's morning bugle call brought me to the surface.

Late nights. Early mornings. Constant travel. Touring was hell. At least Jules and I weren't hung over, which was often more than could be said for the ragtag band that assembled in our suite for breakfast.

"Mags." Julian was holding court at the long banquet table. "Come, my angel of the morning - I've saved you a seat." Fussing around me like a sandfly I wanted to swat, he settled me in front of my boringly predictable bowl of muesli, fresh fruit and yoghurt. I hated breakfast nearly as much as I hated mornings.

"Can't you just behave like a rock star for a moment and be a slug in the mornings? All this cheeriness gives me the shits." I tried to brush stray hair from my eyes; somehow the strands had become stuck to the side of my face and refused to budge.

"Ah, Mags, did you not sleep well?" Jules took in my

disheveled look and motioned to Dan, who was pouring himself a coffee. "IV of caffeine needed over here ASAP."

Dan delivered the duly requested warm brew. The aroma filled my nostrils and I felt the night begin to lose its grasp of my consciousness. A mere two gulps of the bittersweet liquid then forcing me to face the day.

"Jules, just because you can be up at dawn no matter where we are in the world doesn't mean you have to make the rest of us suffer." I picked up my spoon and begrudgingly scooped a morsel of cereal into my mouth.

"Dan, what's the plan for the day?" Undeterred, Julian ploughed on, pushing a glass of orange juice at me and taking control.

Purple was the tour sheet color for this trip. Dan's eccentricity, though that was a much-needed asset when working with a group like ours. As the aubergine paper made its way down the table I remembered we weren't traveling today - we had the luxury of performing three nights in a row in the same city. My spirits lifted.

The day sheet arrived in front of Jules and me:

EURO/ASIA TOUR
SATURDAY 27TH FEBRUARY – PERFORMANCE 2
JULES ON STAGE: 21.15
NOTES:
PLEASE MEET IN THE LOBBY AT 11.15 FOR ROCK CLIMBING.
WE WILL BE BACK BY 15.00 – SO JULES CAN HAVE HIS AFTERNOON NAP.
QUOTE FOR THE DAY:
'THE FIRST THING TO DO WHEN YOU GET UP IN THE MORNING IS SMILE. GET IT OVER WITH.'

WC FIELDS
- DAN AKA 'THE MAN'

Julian poked me in the ribs. "You and WC Fields, huh. He must've hated breakfast as well."

I couldn't help smiling. "This isn't directed at me by any chance, is it, Dan?"

In a moment Dan was by my side. He grasped my hand, planting a kiss on my knuckles. "My dear, dear, Mags. Would I be so bold?"

The gentlemanly gesture and his perfect English enunciation tickled me and I laughed out loud. "Sir, I do believe you would."

"Gawd, listen to the two of them." Frederick picked up a grape and threw it in Dan's direction. "I swear, if we spend much more time performing by that bleeding castle he'll have us all on stage in a full set of armor."

"Now there's an idea." Julian's eyes sparkled.

"Don't even go there." Ted stood up, his chair scraping across the marble tiles. "It's tough enough playing percussion, never mind being forced to wear it."

I pushed my bowl away, only half of the contents eaten. The balance just didn't appeal. "Well, I suppose if you're going to make me clamber up a nasty fake wall I'd better get myself sorted." I stood up, promising myself some time in the seclusion of the bathroom. The other trouble with being on tour - the lack of privacy and alone time. "Don't you lot have somewhere to be?"

Frederick's grape bounced up and down the table as the crew lobbed it from one person to another. I should have been grateful breakfast hadn't degenerated into a full-scale food fight.

16

"They're happy here - aren't you, my people?" Now Julian joined the fray, encouraging Frederick to throw a grape in his mouth.

Time for me to go.

"I don't know how you monkeys do it." Panting, I clung halfway up the sculpted rock face, one foot on a tiny outcrop of yellow plastic, the other precariously placed on a blue piece, with my fingernails feeling as if they were about to snap. My legs quivering from the strain and sweat pricking my face, I decided rock climbing wasn't a sport I'd be taking up any time in the near future.

"Come on, you can do it, Mags." Sheree's encouragement from below reminded me that there were people down there taking in the view of my derriere trussed up in a nasty climbing harness.

"Just don't let go of that rope!" I felt a twinge of vertigo start to set in. I tried not to concentrate on the fact the only thing that lay between me and certain death was the safety rope clipped to my harness, strung through a pulley above me and being held by one of Jules' bodyguards below. I closed my eyes, breathed deeply and waited for the shaking in my legs to subside.

"Grab this red one." Dan's voice drifted into my consciousness.

I opened my eyes and glared at him. "Was this your insane idea?"

"Jules wanted to go skydiving so stop complaining. You could've spent the morning falling out of a perfectly good plane." Dan hauled himself up another couple of colored pegs, leaving me in his harnessed wake.

"Mags! Mags! Mags! Mags!..." The chanting from the

assembled crowd below started to reach an uproarious climax.

I'd been around this particular group long enough to know I'd never live it down if I didn't make the balance of the trek up this damn wall. Driven by the melodic mantra from below, I struck out, and in no time at all found myself clinging to the top rail with Dan to my left and the long-limbed Sheree to my right.

Then I realized the ordeal was only half over.

"Against my better judgment you lot have got me up here. Now how the hell do I get back down?" I was shaking - not only from the exertion, but also from the sheer horror of being perched twenty meters up in the air on a couple of minuscule plastic footrests.

"You can't be scared of heights." Sheree swung off the top bar, almost performing one of her nightly dances, oblivious to the distance between her and terra firma below. "You've just been delivered to a gig by chopper with Jules."

"That's different." I rested my sweating brow on the roughcast wall, grateful to be wearing a helmet. At least my brains wouldn't spill all over the floor when I fell.

"How? You should check out the view - it's awesome." I could tell from the tone of her voice, Sheree didn't understand.

A cheer rose from below us. The signal we could now descend.

"When I'm enclosed by something it's okay. Just me and meters to certain death is another story."

"Well, you can come down now." I almost didn't hear the end of the sentence as Dan vanished, the squeal from his safety line nearly drowning out the last of his words.

"Just sit back on your harness. Like this, like the instructor showed us." Sheree let go of the bar at the top of the wall and sat down, as if there were some invisible chair hanging in midair.

"I can't." I hated myself for being pathetic.

"Yes, you can." Sheree sounded so certain. "I'm here. I'll come down with you."

No amount of coaching could convince me to let go of the secure iron bar at the top of that wall. Sheree begged, she scolded, she played the kind aunt, but despite the logic of it all I simply could not let go. The thought of sitting back into nothing horrified me beyond reason. Even if I had wanted to let go, my hands refused to obey the thoughts that came from my brain.

Trapped and trembling, I started to cry.

My sobs were interrupted and I felt a comforting touch in the middle of my back. I opened one wet eye and met Julian's concerned gaze. A small tuft of chest hair poked provocatively from his V-neck T-shirt, the balance of the material stretched tightly over the bulges in his muscular arms. He was covered in sweat from the exertion of climbing the wall and I could smell his scent. How come I'd never noticed these delightful things about him before? Perhaps the threat of impending death made my senses more acute.

"Come on, Mags." His voice - the same voice I listened to night after night - touched me, caressed me, ran over me like treacle, as I stood petrified on the wall.

"I've tried everything, J. I just can't get her to move." Sheree's voice had the same edge of frustration I'd heard her using with her husband when they fought on the phone.

19

"Why don't you head on down and let them all know she's okay." Julian rubbed my lower back. I hadn't realized how much it was aching until he touched me. "We'll be down in a jiffy, won't we, Mags?"

I nodded, feeling in a dream-like state.

"Good luck." The pulley above Sheree's head shrieked and I imagined her bouncing down the wall.

"You need to let go of the bar." Julian oozed a calm assurance.

"I know." My voice sounded far away. "I want to, I really do, but I just can't."

"You're scared." Julian made it a statement.

"Petrified."

"It's how I feel every night before I go on stage."

I looked across at him. "But you still manage to do it."

"Only with the help of a wonderful woman I know."

I thought about all those nights I stood beside him while he shook and then vomited. "What are you scared of?"

"Everything. All of them. The thousands of people out the front who all want a piece of me, who all think they know me, who believe that because they buy my songs they somehow own a part of me."

He picked at the rough gray surface of the wall. I couldn't help noticing how dusty it was up here.

"So why do you go out there?"

He shrugged. "I ask myself that on a daily basis. I don't know how to do anything else. And I have you all to support. Maybe I just need the fuckers after all. I don't know."

"And you're scared every night?"

He grinned. "Don't you dare tell anyone."

"Most of us know. I didn't realize it could be as bad as

this."

"I'm scared stiff, every night." He reached across and took my right hand from the bar. "Come with me, Mags. Promise me you will always be with me. I don't know if I could do it all otherwise."

An indescribable weight of responsibility - and something else I couldn't quite identify - overshadowed my fear.

"I promise." The two words came out of my mouth without hesitation.

He leaned across the dusty wall. I thought for a moment he was going to kiss me.

"Thank you." He whispered the two simple words in my ear.

I almost wished he had kissed me. Then self-preservation kicked in. "Now, how do I get down?"

"You have to sit back and relax. Do you trust me?"

He knew I did. I nodded.

"Let the other hand go."

My left hand came away from the bar, almost by itself. I leaned back into the harness and allowed the security of Julian's strength to support me.

"No hands, Mags." His right hand came away from the wall and we walked down together, one step at a time, holding hands.

Halfway down the wall we were met by resounding applause and wolf-whistles as the crew below cheered us on. A warmth spread through me. The same feeling I had on a sunny day when I lay on my back on the summer-scorched earth and watched clouds dancing through the trees.

Julian stopped. "You hear that?"

21

"How could I not hear it?"
"That's why I do it every night."

CHAPTER THREE

"We're being taped again tonight so I want to see the best fucking performance we can muster. OK?" Julian had everyone's rapt attention backstage.

The huddle of band and dancers all linked arms around each other, forming a tight circle. Anticipation filled the air.

Then he prayed: "Elvis, grant me the Serenity..."

"Uh-huh..." the group responded.

"To accept the things I cannot change..."

"Uh-huh..." with an accompanying swing of the hips.

"The courage to change the things I can..."

"Uh-huh..." all hips swung in the opposite direction.

"And the wisdom to know the difference."

"Thank you. Thank you."

What had initially been a complete piss-take had somehow morphed into a spiritual ritual. No one was prepared to take to the stage until they'd recited the prayer. It was worse than the roadies insisting on wearing the same pair of "lucky" black pants every night. The show would be doomed if the correct rituals weren't

23

performed.

Sirens sounded. The band's cue to take to the stage. The crowd, whipped into a frenzy of anticipation, erupted as the lights came up and the band launched into its thrumming intro.

Alone with me, Jules went white, shook violently and vomited.

Tonight I understood. I wiped his mouth and kissed him on the forehead. "Thank you for getting me down today."

He smiled. "Thank you for getting me up there every night." Then he hesitated for a moment, turning his attention away from the stage and to me. "I liked looking after you today. I want to do it more often."

The idea of someone looking after me was foreign. I hadn't a clue what to say.

Cue Julian's intro.

"Go get 'em, Jules," I said.

He left me in the wings with my thoughts and went to his followers.

Getting Julian to his customized tour bus through the swarm of dedicated fans outside the hotel's main entrance was the issue next morning.

The double-story coach, emblazoned with his touring logo, had been parked outside the front doors. My preferred method of entry and exit in these situations - the back entrance - had been ruled out by Dan.

"Publicity, Mags. We want him stirring young hearts into a frenzy. It puts bums on seats and pays our wages."

Wages which also needed to be paid to burly

bodyguards in the form of Otis, a huge, black ex-Special-Squad police officer and his sidekick Verne, a muscled ex-military man. They both flanked Jules and were never far away at any given moment when we were out.

Otis and Verne kept the screaming European women far enough away from Jules for him to make it relatively unscathed to the bus. It was like watching Moses part the Red Sea.

Then Julian surprised us all. He took the hand of a slight, dark woman and she followed him quietly into the bus. Verne stood guard at the door, keeping the balance of the fans out, while Otis followed at a discreet distance.

"Mags. He wants you." Verne's unmistakable shriek came to me over the noise of the giddy pack of women.

I ran ahead of Ted, who was making a huge scene of passionately kissing the woman who'd spent the night with him after the show. Frederick, preferring to remain almost anonymous, looked on appalled at the flamboyant display. I slipped past Verne, hurried through the shared lounge and kitchen area with its required supply of coffee, teas and fruit, and caught up with Julian and his raven-haired follower at the foot of the narrow spiral staircase that led to Julian's quiet lounge above. The other half of the second story housed the curtained-off bunk area where I shared on the road sleeping quarters with Sheree, Frederick, Dan and Ted. Otis and Verne had a bunk between them, so someone was always on hand in case we struck any kind of trouble.

"Can you give us ten minutes?" Julian still held the hand of the young woman.

She didn't look like his "type" and my curiosity was piqued. What could she possibly have done outside to attract his attention?   He often seemed impervious to the screams and demands of his fans and I knew he hated not being able to share the obscurity of some of the band and dancers.

While the rest of the band and dancers poured themselves into the second tour bus, I waited downstairs for the girl to leave.

"I didn't think he'd spent any time with anyone here." Sheree curled herself into a tight ball on the sofa. Julian preferred her to travel with us and she enjoyed getting away from the band politics.

"He hasn't. I can't imagine what this girl did to catch his eye."

"How long's she been up there?"   Sheree winked suggestively.

"It's not like that." I grinned back at her. "You know he doesn't bring the deranged stalkers onto the bus."

"No, he just leaves them weeping and wailing in the hotel sheets for you to deal with in the mornings. Honestly, I don't know how you do it, sharing a suite with him - it would drive me insane." Sheree played with her hair, which shone in the morning sunlight.

I'd been left holding the hand of many a sobbing young woman who mistakenly believed, having bedded Julian for a night, that they were going on tour and would become the Yoko to his John.

"Lately he's given up on the girl-after-every-concert routine. He seems to be happy to come back to the hotel and play cards or watch a movie with me." It occurred to me we'd almost fallen into the routine of an old married couple.

"No one out there would believe that." Sheree picked a

banana out of the fruit bowl and spun it in circles. "Least of all Jeremy. He's certain we're all out on the town night after night, partying until dawn." She giggled. "He thinks Jules sniffs coke off the tits of prostitutes on a regular basis. How absurd is that?"

"Insane. Jules' mind is altered enough and he hates drugs. And what makes Jeremy think a teetotaler who has half of the women in the western world trying to get into his trousers would bother with prostitutes?"

We both collapsed in a fit of the giggles. "That's how twisted Jeremy's gotten about this tour." Sheree wiped laughter tears from her eyes. "I just don't know what to do about him anymore. He's really starting to piss me off." Her demeanor turned serious. "How come you don't have these problems with Nick?"

I shrugged. "Nick has his own life. It suits him when I'm away. He gets a chance to deal with his offshore interests without having any guilt about leaving me at home fretting."

"So you're telling me I should be married to an international shipping magnate, not a plumber and gasfitter."

I shrugged again. "I don't know what to tell you. He's either going to deal with your lifestyle on the road or he's not."

I wasn't going to tell her the truth about my marriage - it suited me for the band to think it was perfect. No one needed to know how unhappy I was when I wasn't on tour. "You know, Shez, Nick and I have never had the nine-to-five life. Even before I started working for Jules my life always changed from one week to the next."

Sheree looked pained, intense concentration etched

onto her face as the enormity of my words worked their way through her head. "I suppose it's why Nick can cope with Jules' demands when you're home, yeah?"

I nodded, though I knew it was mainly because Nick didn't seem to care. I thought about the number of times Julian had phoned and demanded I drop everything to accompany him on some obscure mission. The most recent ones seemed to revolve around finding perfect pieces of designer furniture for his latest apartment.

I ran my usual cover line, even though I was almost tempted to share with Sheree the difficulties of living with Nick's debilitating periods of depression. "Nick has always demanded that I make my own way in the world, be my own person and not rely on him. He's adamant that a healthy relationship is about two people building their own lives and their own independence yet choosing to be with each other. He enjoys hearing the insane stories about what happens on tour."

It still made me uncomfortable, only telling half the truth. Nick had been schooled in the "what happens in the marriage stays inside the marriage" camp. He made it clear that presentation of a perfect couple to the outside world was paramount.

Sheree continued to twirl the banana on the tabletop. I rattled on, trying to convince myself that this kind of a marriage suited me.

Though the longer I stayed on this particular tour, the more unpalatable my home life seemed to me. What had changed? Then I thought about the caring way Jules helped me down from the rock wall and what he'd said before the show.

"You're lucky. Jeremy seems to have this insane idea

that he works hard and therefore I should be at home when he gets in.   Have the dinner on the table, all that kind of 1950s bullshit."   She sighed.

"You must have known he had these views before you got married."   Had I known that living with Nick would become almost unbearable?

Tears sprang to Sheree's eyes and she shook her head. "No, he loved my dancing.   It's just since I've been on this tour that he's changed."

"So you didn't have these problems last year.   With the last tour, I mean?"

"No."

She looked so miserable I just wanted to cuddle her. How could I advise her not to make the same mistake I'd made?   Marriage wasn't supposed to be this hard, surely?

"Can you work out what's changed then?   Besides you two getting married?"

Sheree thought about it for a while.   "I suppose if I'm honest he just barely tolerated me touring last year.   Kept talking about when we'd settle down and how once his business was doing really well I wouldn't have to go off into the night."

"So it's not just this tour then?"

"No," now she began to sob.   I crossed the bus to collect a box of tissues and bumped into Julian just as he was showing his little dark follower out.   She was wearing his tour jacket.   We had a spare for him in the back, but she must have really touched him for him to give up a jacket.

Verne climbed on board.   I saw Otis gave him the thumbs up and the hydraulic doors closed with a hiss.   We were on our way.

Julian spotted Sheree with a handful of tissues and

immediately dropped down into the couch next to her.

"What's the matter, gorgeous?" He looked at me as Sheree continued to cry. "Can I help?"

Had Nick ever asked me if he could help when I sat sobbing like Sheree? I didn't think so.

I shook my head at Julian and made eyes at the staircase behind me. Mysteriously, the rest of the crew were hanging at the back of the bus, leaving me to my counseling session.

Jules kissed Sheree on the crown of her head. "I'll be upstairs if you need me - OK, kiddo?"

Sheree nodded and Julian pushed the box of tissues closer to her as he made to leave. "Looks like you'll be needing plenty of these, Mags."

I grabbed his arm, before he could leave us. I still had an overwhelming desire to know why he'd taken that young woman upstairs. I'd begun to see things about Jules I'd not noticed before. He genuinely cared about people.

"What did that girl say to you?"

He smiled. "She quoted an obscure lyric from the sixth track on the Moonlight album."

"What, wasn't that your fifth album?"

"Second, actually."

"I don't know how you can remember them all." We were touring on the back of his ninth and most days he spent some time working on songs for the next. I was blown away he could recall which song came from what album.

"Hours of sweat, Mags. Hours of sweat and torment in the hands of the producer from hell." He polished his perfectly manicured fingernails on his T-shirt. "Have you got another tour jacket for me somewhere?"

30

"Yes, I'll find it. But plenty of people quote lyrics at you. I still don't know why that girl was different."

He smiled. "She understood the pain I felt when I wrote those words. The song helped her through a really tough time and she wanted to thank me." His eyes glazed over again and I knew he was back in his past, back in the pain. No one could connect with him when he went there.

Julian snapped out of it, a cheery grin bringing him into to the present moment.

I wagged a motherly finger at him. "Well, no more giving away tour jackets. Dan'll have a fit about you blowing the budget."

He half-smiled at me. "No probs, Mags, I'll just steal yours."

Julian's cheek brought a touch of light to Sheree's tear-stained face.

"I think I need a lie down." She looked up at Julian. "She's worn me out, making me think about things."

A flash of concern crossed Julian's features and he sat down again next to Sheree. "What's to think about? Don't you just have the best time out there on stage with me?"

"I do, J. That's the problem."

He looked puzzled. "How can it be a problem to be up there every night, winding forty thousand plus people into a frenzy? The fans love you, Shez. You and I can turn a crowd into a hormonal hotbed in thirty seconds. Where else do you have that kind of power?"

"Nowhere."

Jules tilted her chin toward him with a soft and gentle movement. She looked up, brown eyes doe-like, into his dark green ones. "You don't want to leave me, you don't

31

have to leave me. Let Jeremy get over himself. He's jealous of your talent and of what you have. Don't give your life away for someone else. You'll never forgive yourself."

I felt like he was talking directly to me, not to Shez.

With that, he picked himself up and headed for the staircase at the back of the bus. "Mags, I'm writing. I don't want to be disturbed."

My cue to make my way up after him. As Sheree and I moved toward the rear of the bus, the balance of the crew, their eyes on the vacant couch, traded places with us.

Frederick, Ted and Dan entertained themselves when we were on the road with hours of card games. That was, of course, when Frederick wasn't upstairs with Jules agonizing over song composition. Otis and Verne took up their positions at the front doors, constantly on guard. I often wondered when they weren't; they were so devoted to ensuring Jules stayed safe.

There'd been a hideous security breach on tour last year when a deranged fan managed to get backstage in the middle of the show. He lunged at Jules, pushing him into Frederick, and there was a terrifying moment when we realized he could have had a gun or a knife. It wasn't Otis' fault - venue security hadn't been up to standard - but he'd taken it hard. Shortly after that Verne came on the scene, and there'd been no security breaches since.

Together they worked what they called close-proximity security. Basically it meant that when we were on tour they never left Julian's side. When we weren't on tour they contracted themselves out to government officials or international visitors who needed protection. Absurdly, they preferred the touring life with Jules. They felt as if they belonged to one huge dysfunctional family and we were grateful to have them on board.

I climbed the small circular staircase to Jules' private retreat. A right turn at the top of the stairs took me to the narrow door. A "Do not disturb - genius at work" sign hung over the doorknob. Sheree turned left and headed for one of the curtained-off bunk areas - the nearest thing the rest of us had to uninterrupted privacy while on the road.

I knocked on Jules' door and went in.

Jules sat in the middle of his double bed, guitar laid lazily across his knee, scribbling lyrics in a large, spiral-bound notebook.

"Hey, Mags."

He dropped the pen on top of the Egyptian cotton sheets and started strumming the guitar. He closed his eyes and began to sing.

Chasing the elusive moment of truth,
Wasted minutes of exuberant youth,
It's all been left behind,
The missing fragments of my mind.

I picked up the fine felt-nibbed pen and put it on the notebook. I spent hours on tour trying to find Laundromats that specialized in ink removal. Julian insisted it was the price we paid for creativity and I should just buy new ones.

I took up my station in the corner of the room, on the built-in couch, and pulled my laptop from its case. My lifeline to the outside world hummed into life. To my left was a miniature bench full of fruit and chocolate with a petite bar fridge beneath. The coffee machine above waited patiently for me to begin the ritual of making coffee for us both. To my right, through another slim door, lay Julian's compact bathroom. The trade-off for me keeping it clean meant I could share it with him and didn't need to use the communal soak-pit below.

Flicking the switch on the coffee machine, as I waited for it to warm up I watched the industrial cityscape give way to suburbia - lots of little picture-perfect homes standing shoulder to shoulder with their symmetrical driveways running down to perfectly proportioned roadways. Juvenile trees, a landscape architect's attempt to soften the hard lines, positioned at regular intervals between the concrete, tile and plaster.

I wondered about the people who lived in those homes. What kind of a life did they lead? Why couldn't I live a simple suburban life?

What had once been lush, productive farmland was now smothered beneath concrete and tar seal. Only small blisters of green in the form of tiny, perfectly manicured lawns had escaped the onslaught.

I shuddered and turned my mind back to the coffee-making. Jules sang on behind me, oblivious to our travel, lost in the world of his musical mind.

With due care I placed a long black on the small unit by Julian's side. He acknowledged the coffee with a tiny tilt of his head, never breaking from the rhythmic strumming and singing.

I settled back down with my laptop, opened my mail account and waited to see what horrors from the outside world lurked in my inbox. While we traveled, while Jules wrote, I had a chance to catch up with my correspondence, both tour related and personal.

There were twenty-eight new emails. Seven of them

were personal, including a short note from Nick letting me know he'd arrived safely in Dubai. He'd be there for the next two weeks, preparing and networking for a trade show. He was due to leave just days before the tour hit South-East Asia but the email said he wasn't going to delay his departure so he could meet up with us. I harbored huge guilt because of the relief I felt at not having to meet with him.

The other twenty-one emails were work related.

"The web boys want a blog as part of the tour update," I told Julian.

Jules looked up from his scribbling. "You'd better write one then."

I sighed. "It's supposed to come from you."

"I'm busy."

It was no use arguing with him; I'd tried on many occasions. "They want photos as well. What shall we write about?"

He put his guitar down. "I hate this shit."

"Remember Dan's mantra."

"I know, I know." He looked pained. "Bums on seats."

I had his attention so I pressed on, opening a word-processing document to type as we talked.

"How long have we been on the road?" he asked.

I took a quick look at the calendar. "Thirty-seven days."

"It seems like forever." Julian rolled his eyes. "How many shows have we done?"

"Hmm, thirty-seven days, that's thirty six nights, with six nights off. Thirty."

"No wonder I'm exhausted." He flopped onto his back.

"Stop being a drama queen."

He sat up, grinning. "Only another eight shows before we get a whole week off. What will I do with myself if I'm not on stage every night?"

"Sarcasm doesn't become you." I glanced up at him over the laptop screen. He looked almost child-like, hair mussed up and behaving badly. I had a sudden urge to kiss him.

My conscience screamed in horror and I tried to turn my mind back to work. "Where's that photographer when I need him? Don't move, you look perfect."

He looked more than perfect. Suddenly he'd started to look incredibly appealing.

"I don't want that pesky bastard in here." Julian's eyes darkened.

"Rather here than at home. You know you're public property when we're on tour, so stop misbehaving."

I opened the door and shot down the stairs. Frederick and Ted were playing cards with the photographer.

"Just the boys I need." The three of them looked up from their game, perplexed. "Sorry to interrupt, lads, but I need some shots for the blog. Jules looks gorgeous and I want you to get him before his mood changes."

Used to being shooed away from the object of his pictorial desires, Colin dropped his cards and nearly leaped over the seat to where he'd stowed his camera case.

"Frederick, I need you too. Where's your guitar?"

"Jeez, Mags, can't we do this later?" Ted looked pissed off. "I've got a great hand."

"Tough luck, mate." Frederick gave him a hearty back-slap. "The boss needs us. Just reshuffle the deck and we'll be back with you in a jiffy."

"I thought he was writing, Mags. This is just not on."

Ted's pained expression made me giggle. "And it's not a laughing matter. I haven't had a decent hand in days."

I patted him on the shoulder in what I hoped was a soothing fashion. "Sorry, Ted. You know what *he-who-shall-be-obeyed* can be like."

"Right, I'm ready." Colin skipped from foot to foot at the bottom of the stairs, camera in hand.

"You can download direct to my laptop from that camera?"

Colin nodded.

"Perfect." I'd have the blog up in no time.

I herded the two excited men up the stairs and blew the still seething Ted a kiss. He gave me the finger.

Julian was scribbling down more lyrics as the three of us squeezed ourselves into his tiny sanctuary.

"I told you not to move."

Jules looked up, his face a mask of innocence. I heard the click of the camera behind me. Colin preserving the moment in time for perpetuity.

Frederick settled himself on the far side of Julian's wide bed, his back to us and the camera. "What have you got down so far?"

The creative energy in the room ratcheted up a notch and Julian started to play and sing. Colin buzzed the room like a snap-happy hummingbird.

All the hair on the back of my neck stood on end.

CHAPTER FOUR

Hours later I left Jules and Frederick - still deep in discussion on their latest collaboration - and headed downstairs. I'd finished the blog piece and our photographer had long since been ushered out the door. He was leaving the tour at the next city, and most of us happy to see the back of him and his intrusive lens.

A photojournalist, he'd negotiated a deal with Dan to cover the tour and then write a book. Jules had been less than enthusiastic and had insisted on complete artistic control. If there was anything he didn't like it wouldn't get printed. Julian's terms also limited Colin's time with us to the first part of the tour. After that he'd be sending me daily copy and photos via email for approval. The prospect of daily confrontations with Jules over them didn't appeal to me in the slightest.

A frantic "Stop the bus!" came from behind me and I jerked around losing my place in the book I was reading and instantly transported from the terror of death row to my own preferred prison.

Jules was running down the length of the bus yelling, "I

want to get out of here. Stop the bus. Let me off."

Otis caught my eye, a puzzled look etched on his features.

I shrugged and mouthed, "I have no idea."

I moved forward to where Jules was standing over the driver, wildly gesticulating and saying, "Pull over here."

"I can't, there wouldn't be enough space for the traffic to get by." The driver looked to me for assistance. I had nothing.

Otis and I now flanked a very agitated Julian.

"What's up, man?" Otis planted a firm hand on Jules shoulder, the spread of his large palm spanning from the base of Julian's neck to the edge of his arm.

At the touch I noticed Julian's nervous state begin to lessen. He looked across the top of that huge hand to me.

"I need to get off, Mags. We've been stuck in this fucking tin can for hours. Can't I have just ten minutes outside?"

"Otis, what do you think?" We had no scheduled stops; the idea was always to get us to the next destination as soon as possible. I knew Otis would have checked with the driver how we were getting to the next city; it was part of his job keeping Julian secure, being aware of any threat along the way.

"There's a rest stop just down the highway on the right. We could stop there for a while."

He unhanded Jules who immediately gave me a kiss on the crown of my head. "I knew you could sort it out for me, Mags."

Less than ten minutes later we were parked in the pleasant surrounds of a highway rest stop. A sweeping gravel road ran off the main highway and deposited weary travelers in the middle of a sublimely cool, wooded world. Everyone piled off the bus and into the damp, chilly air as the second bus came to a halt behind us.

Jules took a deep breath and exhaled theatrically. "Ahh! This is much better than that air-conditioned tank. We should stop more often."

Verne shadowed Jules while Otis quickly scouted out the miniature parkland.

After listening to a message from Otis, Verne told Jules, "You should stretch your legs. There's a stream just up ahead with a bridge."

"Come on, Mags. Let's go for a walk." Jules took my hand and led me toward what appeared to be a walking track. As we left the roadside clearing I was overcome by the sweet scent of the woodlands. There was a rustle in the trees ahead of us. I waited for some exotic creature to appear on the track, only to see the bulk of Otis appear from the gloom.

He gave me the universal okay with his thumb and forefinger and retreated behind us, to blend into the shadows with Verne. I'd gotten used to never being quite alone when I traveled with Jules. Otis and Verne were like the mythical *elephant-in-the-living-room*. Always there, but never talked about.

"Hang on." Jules dropped my hand and moved toward a large tree.

As I instinctively went with him he started pulling at the buckle on his jeans. "Just need a pee." He grinned at me, a look of childish delight on his face.

"You could have gone on the bus." I felt like his mother some days.

"Nah! More fun in the outdoors."

40

I dropped back, in time to hear the snapping of a fast shutter behind me.   As I turned around I saw an entourage trailing us and our photographer swooping down on Jules, like a game hunter in for the kill.

Anger flashed hot in an instant and I grabbed the camera. "Get that thing out of here!"

Jules pivoted his upper body, still peeing on the tree, the same look of mischief on his face. "Leave him be, Mags."

The shocked photographer, realizing he was being given permission to continue, recovered instantly and started shooting again.

I stormed past Jules up the track and left them all to it.

Blazing with rage, I barely noticed the beauty of my surroundings.   I covered the short distance to the bridge and trotted over it like a Billy Goat Gruff on speed.

The steep zigzag track beyond was no match for my fury. I arrived at a perfectly proportioned gazebo, panting as if I'd just run a mile under three minutes, and dropped onto the hard wooden seat.

To my dismay I discovered tears were trickling down my cheeks. With impatience I brushed them away. Julian infuriated me and I wasn't even sure why. I just knew I needed some time on my own.   Something difficult to come by on tour.

"Jesus, Mags. What's gotten into you?"   An out of breath Julian had arrived, red-faced, at the gazebo entrance.

"Fuck off!"

He doubled over, hands resting on his knees, his back rising and falling rapidly as he sucked air into his gasping lungs. "I practically had to run up this frigging track. What's gotten up your arse?"

"You."

He looked up, bewildered. "What have I done?"

"You know exactly what you've done."

"I don't."

"Jules, I'm not an idiot."

He came and sat down next to me and took my hand in his. "I know you're not an idiot."

"I thought I told you to go away." I didn't want him to see I'd been crying. Being around him had become confusing. I didn't trust what I felt anymore.

"I'm not going anywhere until you tell me what this is all about."

"We haven't got time. We should be on the road." I made to stand up but he dragged me back down. Our bodies were pressed together in the small overgrown space. Another overwhelming desire to escape came over me.

"I'm going nowhere 'til this is sorted. What the hell's going on with you?"

I wriggled free and stood up, desperately trying to get some space between us, but his movements mirrored mine. We were still far too close, his proximity, the feelings, all flustering me. I burst into a fresh set of tears.

He pulled me close, hugging me while I sobbed against his chest.

I let him stroke my hair. I was tired. Far too tired. Tired of the chaos, of the bullshit, and of life on the road.

"Come on, Mags. This isn't like you."

He was right. I was the trooper. The staunch no-nonsense organizer. The one who could deal with anything.

Except how I was feeling at the moment.

I sniffed, wiped my nose on my sleeve and pulled myself away from Jules so I could sit back down again. The tears felt cool and strange on my face. Crying wasn't something I often indulged in.   Nor was being emotionally vulnerable.

"I'm sick of the bullshit." I looked Jules straight in the eye.

"Bullshit's part of touring. You know that."

How could I tell him I didn't like him making so much of his body available to the public? And why had that started to bother me now? "You could be a bit more discreet."

"Discreet!" He laughed at me. "This is rock 'n' roll, Mags. It don't understand discreet."

"Well, you should." Anger returned. Along with confusion. I was being an idiot; even I could see that.

"We're in the business of selling dreams, Mags. Don't ever forget that. You can't mix me, the man, with Julian the product."

"It doesn't have to turn you into some sort of idiot pissing on the side of the road." I felt tears prickling at my eyes again and turned my face away so he couldn't see.

He squatted in front of me, looking up into my damp eyes. He caught a single tear on his fingernail. It sat there, a tiny, perfect bubble of me on the end of his ring finger.

Looking across his raised hand, he put my tear in his mouth, his unblinking eyes daring me to protest in some way. A surge of heat ran through me.

In my peripheral vision I caught sight of Otis. I looked over to him and he turned his back on us.

I stood up. "We need to get back." My voice sounded

rough. Emotional.

"We need to talk."

"There's nothing more to talk about." I hurried away from him, thankful we were on tour and surrounded by people.

He rushed after me. "Mags, I know you feel this thing between us."

"You don't know what *you* feel in any given moment - that's why you need me on hand twenty-four, seven. So how the hell could you know what I feel?" I sounded bitter and spiteful and I didn't like that.

"Don't you like being with me?"

"You know I love being with you. But I can't be with you."

He stopped then.

Let me get ahead of him. Let me get away from him.

I'd heard somewhere that a man eventually falls in love with a woman he's attracted to and that a woman becomes more strongly attracted to a man she loves.

I knew three things.

One, I was tired.

Two, I was only one of the many women who loved him.

Three, I was a married woman.

How long could I manage the narrowing distance between us?

CHAPTER FIVE

I marched back onto the bus and threw myself on a seat next to Sheree. "How do you do it?"

"Do what?"   She looked at me, her eyes red-rimmed from crying.

"Keep all those men at arm's length when you spend your nights gyrating all over the stage?"

She shrugged. "Jeremy doesn't believe I do."

"He's an idiot." I saw a chance to bury my own troubles and help someone else. "Have you been crying all morning?"

A sob escaped her. "Yes." She rubbed her nose again and I realized how much pain my dear friend was in.

"Oh, Shez. Come here. Tell me what's going on."

Sheree leaned her liquid frame against me and sobbed into my jacket. Big, gulping sobs. I stroked her sleek hair and waited for the emotional storm to subside. It seemed as if half the women on tour were having nervous breakdowns all at the same time.

"Jeremy's been on the phone again."   She spoke through convulsive sobs.   "He's convinced I must be having affairs or-" her face turned damning "-what does he call them? Oh yes, encounters." The word sounded hard, like a pebble she'd spat out of her mouth.

"What kind of encounters?"

"One-night stands, I guess." Pain flickered across her even features.

I felt a different kind of pain every time I thought about Nick. He paled into the grainy black-and-white part of my life when I was on tour. Everything here was Technicolor, larger than life, and multidimensional. This must be what Jeremy sensed and it frightened him.

It became clear to me that Nick didn't sense the same thing because he simply didn't care - about me or our loveless marriage.

"But you're not cheating on him so he doesn't have anything to worry about. You're probably the most loyal spouse here," I said.

"Aside from you."

I had visions of my last few moments with Jules. A sharp ache, acute and tangible, speared my gut. I pushed the guilty memory aside and tried to concentrate on Sheree. I moved away from her, almost as if on a subconscious level I thought putting some distance between us would help to keep my emerging feelings safe.

"Don't put me on a pedestal here. Everyone has clay feet."

Concern registered in the corners of her eyes.

"But you and Nick are solid as a house. Yeah?"

I nodded. I daren't say a word in case my voice trembled.

"And he never accuses you of cheating or misbehaving when you're away?"

"No." Though I began to wonder what Nick got up to during the months he spent abroad.

"So how come I get accused of sleeping with every man who looks at me?" I could hear the anger and outrage rising in her voice. Feel the heat of indignation radiating off her body.

"I can't answer that for you, Shez. We all know you're devoted. But you've got to understand that for anyone looking in from the outside this kind of life looks like a series of long, drunken, drugged-filled orgies."

"And his lordship getting his dick out on the side of the road doesn't help."

Jules walked by at that moment, his face flushing as he comprehended Sheree's words. He had the good grace to hurry upstairs, but I didn't miss the importance of the fleeting, lost look in his eyes.

"It's publicity, Shez. You know that." Here I was defending his actions when fifteen minutes ago I wanted to throttle him.

"But it doesn't help my cause." She sounded whiny and selfish.

"You're part of the publicity machine. If Jeremy can't cope, then it seems to me you have a simple choice to make." Did I have a simple choice to make? Could it be that easy?

She looked dumbstruck. "You mean..."

I nodded. "Yes, I mean you have to decide what's more important to you - your entertaining life or your married life. From where I'm sitting, it looks as if you've tried to combine the two and Jeremy just isn't able to deal with it."

Tears began to well in her eyes again. "I...I don't think I could make that choice."

Could I?

I leaned over and gave her another hug. "Well, I guess you're just going to have to think about it for a while."

That, I knew, was the other problem with being on tour. Far too much time to think. And I was running out of things to occupy my mind, because I didn't want to think either.

I managed to avoid being alone with Jules before we got to the next hotel. Tired and overwhelmed with guilt, I attached myself to Sheree, determined to help her feel better, even if I couldn't.

Worrying about her kept at bay my sickening realization that the love and devotion between Sheree and Jeremy was startlingly absent from my own marriage. Nick's and my crumbling relationship sat on the marital equivalent of The San Andreas fault and the plates were moving. Touring and the hectic relationship of our lives might have kept the spotlight away from the underlying cracks but I could no longer ignore them.

Pulling up at the front door of the hotel saw the usual circus of media and gaggle of women awaiting Jules' arrival. Somehow the chaos comforted me. I had people and things to organize.

Ted set about ushering the unruly mob on the stairs into some sort of order. Moses might have had an easier job parting the Red Sea. Out of the bus window I could see luggage being pulled from the bowels of the vehicle and carried by poor, straining hotel staff up the stairs. They beat a path through the throng, depositing their load onto trolleys that sat just inside the impressive oak doors. Impressive oak doors that bespoke the five-star-luxury-hotel promise of decadence and delight in the way only exclusive hotel entrances can.

"Right. That's everyone off except Julian." Otis wasn't only speaking to me, but also into the small headpiece that permanently adorned his right ear. Verne, I knew, would be stationed at the front door, waiting for us to disembark.

"I'll get him." I climbed the stairs to his room, wondering what state I'd find him in.

He was sitting on the bed, looking out the window at the sea of people below.

"We need to go," I told him. "Everyone's waiting for you."

"I can see that." His voice sounded flat.

Monotone.

Listless.

"Come sit with me for a minute, Mags."

"Jules." Panic set in, clutching my stomach in a tight embrace.

"We're good, Mags. You don't have to worry."

Reluctantly I sat beside him, aware for the first time of gauging the correct distance between us. Too close and I could inflame the situation, too far and it was obvious I was trying to stay away. In that moment I hated myself.

"We've got a tour to get through. Can't we just agree to concentrate on that for now?" I said.

He nodded. "I wanted to be liked, but not liked this much. I can't go anywhere, I can't be myself. I've forgotten who me is."

I wanted to touch him. To tousle his hair. To tickle him. See him smile.

"I mean, it's terrifying. All these people dependent on me. They've created this monster. A Julian I don't even know. All I ever wanted to do was sing. Make people smile." He turned and looked at me, green eyes boring through me. "Make them love me."

Like the thousands he sang to every night, I sat under his spell, in awe and wonder. Utterly in love with him.

I chose my words with care. "I watch you on stage, making love to thousands. How am I supposed to deal with that?"

Jules shrugged. "It's my job, you know that's not who I am." He held my gaze. Steady. His eyes never leaving mine for a moment. "If you can't cope with it, you should go. No one's going to stop you."

I didn't want to go. He knew that. "Who's going to get you off the bus and on stage?"

"Today it would be wonderful if I didn't have to get on stage."

"Well, you do. So let's go."

I stood up and took his hand in mine and led him downstairs the same way I had thousands of times before. We walked together into the frenzy of our world.

Jules stepped out in front of me, sheltering in behind the bulk of Verne. Otis took Jules' place, following up at the rear of me and the four of us, assisted by Dan's continued shepherding of the crowd, made our way up the stairs to the doors of the hotel.

"Julian! Julian! Over here!"

It was nothing new. The screams from the press. The general tussle. And the weeping and hysterics from women who'd stood here for hours waiting for him. But it took its toll. I hated hotel entrances and exits. I could only imagine what it must be like for Jules.

The crowd closed up claustrophobically behind us, funneling the small group up the stairs. We rode atop of chaos, celebrity flotsam on a sea of emotional fans and demanding media.

Then Jules did something strange and out of character. He stopped at the top of the stairs. Otis had his hand over the lens of a marauding media-type.

"Leave him be, let him get his shot." Jules made the command and Otis stepped away, dropping his hand. Otis and Verne scanned the crowd for any kind of threat. Finger to his lips, Jules motioned for the crowd to be quiet. They obeyed almost instantly.

An eerie silence fell upon those assembled. All I could hear was the quiet clicks of a multitude of cellphone cameras.

I shivered, but I wasn't cold.

Jules began to speak. "We're here for a couple of days. I've given those of you who want to take a picture a chance to do that."

I could no longer hear the phone cameras. The shot taken, the press had dropped their cameras, intent on listening to Julian's message.

He looked down at the fans in front of him. "Are you girls all coming to the show?"

There was an unintelligible scream in response.

"If I spend some time with you all now, will you promise to leave me alone for the next few days?"

I was hit by another incomprehensible wall of sound, which I took to be a further response in the positive.

Jules turned to me. "Mags, I need a pen for signing shit. Have the boys get everyone organized into some kind of line."

"What are you going to sign? I haven't got any promo gear - it's all back stage." I dug around in my bag and found a black marker pen.

"I'll sign their bloody tits if that'll buy me some peace for the next few days."

I couldn't help giggling. "Well, that's indelible ink so be very careful."

He threw me a mischievous grin. "Right. Now who's first and what have you got for me to sign?"

Otis and Verne knew the drill and began corralling the excited girls into an orderly line. The press hung around like vultures over a dying carcass, looking for another shot to sell.

Jules had occasionally run impromptu autograph sessions before and it was a two-edged sword. The girls accumulated because they knew sometimes they'd get special attention. On the upside, one of them would now post the outcome of today's stalking on the fan-blog and not so many would come for a while.

Jules would get his requested peace, because they were having a piece of him now.

I stood in the shadows of his fame, as so many of us did, watching the adoring public fawn and faint. I thought about the day as he autographed T-shirts and hats, thighs and underwear. Was nothing sacred?

These young women were so willing to sell themselves to him. They'd be back tonight, haunting the bar, hoping an autograph this afternoon was enough to get them an invite into his bed tonight. I wanted to tell them they had no idea who he was. I wanted to tell them his heart wasn't in it.

I wanted to tell them he was mine.

But these young women were the lifeblood of the huge industry which was Julian. I, on the other hand, was but a tiny cog in the wheels of that immense machine. A tiny, married cog, I reminded myself. If I bucked in the traces I would simply be disposed of.

Swiftly.

Silently.

CHAPTER SIX

The long afternoon stretched ahead of us and I tried to relax before the show. Through the double doors of the suite I caught a glimpse of Jules lifting weights. He was standing in front of a large gilt mirror lifting a couple of purple dumbbells. With his back to me, not only was I accosted by the splendor of his nakedness, but I had the pleasure of an uninterrupted view of both sides of his beautiful body.

Jules worked hard at keeping himself fit. Hours on stage demanded a high level of aerobic fitness, but he also liked to keep his muscles tight so the resistance work had become a part of his daily routine.

I daren't move. I didn't want to alert him to my presence; neither did I want to leave. I found myself unable to tear my eyes from the magnificence of his rippling frame. I almost felt like one of the repulsive paparazzi who hounded us. The only thing missing was a camera and I wouldn't need a telephoto lens at this distance. Still, I couldn't move.

Jules continued his flexing and stretching routine, the

individual muscles in his arms tensing and relaxing. His weights regime looked like some kind of bizarre choreographed scene from a ballet.

I had an uninterrupted view of Julian's genitals. Not that I hadn't seen his genitalia before - he had no qualms about walking naked around the suite, or backstage, or in the recording studio for that matter. But I found myself studying him. I felt like a pervert, but I also sensed myself becoming aroused. A delicious tension began to build deep inside of me.

Julian now lay down on the floor on his back, arms outstretched, the purple weights pinning his arms to the floor. A sheen of light sweat embraced his body. His strong, muscular chest with its sea of dark hair gave way to the concave plane of his belly. A strip of dark hair parted at his navel before traveling to meet the thick curls that caressed his cock.

I had the desire to mount him.

Julian grimaced, bringing the weights up off the floor, his entire chest area heaving with the effort.

I wanted to make him grimace like that. I wanted to feel his body tense and hard underneath me. I sensed my nipples peak. He started to grunt as he struggled to lift the weights.

I started to get wet.

"Ten thousand screaming blonde women and you're back on top. Yeah!" Dan gave Jules a high-five as they walked back from his second encore.

The crowd were still screaming for more, but the house lights had gone up - the signal Jules would not be back on stage again.

55

"How was that? How fucking cool was that?" Jules bounced around backstage on a post-show high. The crowd had warmed to him and he'd enjoyed himself. It didn't happen often, but when it did an electrical surge ran through the backstage crew.

"Get everyone in my room." Jules cantered through the labyrinth of backstage hallways like a Lipizzaner pony. I followed in his wake, impossible feelings of gloom weighing heavy on my shoulders.

The band and dancers, all as high as Jules from the show, packed into his dressing room. The atmosphere hummed around them all. Why any of them ever needed drugs when they had this remained a mystery to me.

"Excellent show. Excellent show." Jules held court over the entire group. They stood in awe of him, as did the ten thousand they had all just performed for.

"Could you feel them? Could you feel them all?" Jules' eyes blazed.

The crew's eyes all had the same euphoric stare.

"When you asked them all to stand on the seats." Ted's excited voice filled the small space.

"And they bloody well did!" Frederick entered the fray.

"It was magic. And you, my gorgeous darling..." Jules turned his attention to Sheree, holding his hand out to her. She took it and joined him, standing beside him. His princess. "You were dynamite."

Sheree tucked herself into Jules' body, the way she did on stage. They were a perfect fit.

My body reacted physically, before my brain even had a chance to work out what I was feeling. I wanted to tear them apart. These overpowering feelings of a right to ownership of Jules were killing me.

Sheree had the temerity to blush, she who'd writhed in ecstasy only moments before with him on stage. I understood in that instant how Jeremy must be feeling. Bile began to rise in my throat. Insidious jealousy stalked me for the first time in my life.

"It's nothing, Jules - you make it all so easy."

She even used my name for him. No one else called him Jules, only me.

I loved Sheree, but in that split second I wanted to rip her apart, piece by gorgeous piece.

He kissed her on the forehead, let her go, and then swatted her butt as she stepped away from him.

"Right," Dan said, "let's get moving guys and gals. We've earned a night out on the tiles and I'm sure our appreciative audience is already making their way back to the hotel bar." He started to usher people out of the door. "If you're not on the coach in ten minutes we're going without you."

I felt like Cinderella, but somehow I'd missed the ball and was still wearing two shoes. Prince Charming pulled off his sodden shirt and dropped it on a nearby table. He snapped the tab on a can of energy drink.

Caffeine. Another hit. After a show like this one I knew it'd be a long night.

I watched him chug the contents. The sharp contrast of his jawbone pointing to the heavens, his Adam's apple rising and falling with each hurried gulp, the muscular line of his frame, and his skin still blushed with the exertion of performance.

I tore my eyes away, concentrating on finding a fresh, clean shirt from the rack. My fingers shook as I fought with the fine linen, the buttons stubbornly refusing to slip through tailor-made buttonholes.

"Here, you need to put this on so we can go." I handed him the shirt, keeping my eyes downcast. I suddenly wished the room was full again with his followers. Part of me longed to be alone with him; the other part sat scared in the corner, trying to work out how to escape.

"You coming out tonight, Mags?" His tone was soft. Loving. Terrifying.

"You...you're going out?" Confusion made me stutter.

"Yes, and I'd like you to come with me." He pulled the shirt on, oblivious to my discomfort at being asked.

"You never go out after a show."

"After a night like tonight the crew would never forgive me if I didn't at least show my face. How could I not go out with the lads?"

"Uhm, I don't know."

"So, you'll come?" His hand came to my chin, lifting my face up so I had to look him in the eyes. "You know I want you."

His fingers trailed their way across my cheek and down the side of my neck, coming to rest behind my ear. I shivered as the electrical pulse from his touch registered. The words hung in the air between us. A flicker crossed Jules' face for a second, almost as if he'd heard his own words for the first time.

"No. I'll stay in." He'd created turmoil in my nicely ordered world.

"Please, babe."

His voice made my body ache. I'd never refused him anything before. "I can't come, Jules." I turned away from his touch, my neck still hot where his fingers had caressed my cool skin.

He shrugged, almost as if he were shrugging away the intimacy we'd shared. "Ah, well, it's your loss. I suppose you and Shez'll have a cup of tea and phone your husbands."

I looked back at him, my hand instinctively touching my neck where his hand had been only a second ago. He might as well have slapped me.

Jules stared me down, his eyes intense, taunting me, daring me to say something.

"Why are you trying to hurt me?"

"Just pointing out the facts." His voice cracked, and it wasn't from the evening's vocal performance. "You need to make a choice and I guess you have. You're staying in."

He walked out the door ahead of me, his voice echoing back down the subterranean passage. "I'll see you on the bus."

I'd spent the night alone in the hotel suite, too wound up to sleep. Jules hadn't come back. Everyone was out, including Sheree, enjoying the victorious fruits of their labor.

For most of the band that meant copious supplies of alcohol and drugs, topped off with a never-ending supply of eager men and women happy to engage in whatever sexual depravity they desired.

I must have fallen asleep in front of the flat-screen TV, its mind-numbing documentaries acting like some kind of sedative.

I'd no idea how long I dozed, but eventually I heard the unmistakable sound of Jules and some bimbo he'd picked up from around town arriving back. High-pitched laughter filtered through the suite. My stomach lurched; I wanted to be sick.

Jules stopped dead in his tracks when he saw me on the couch. He turned to the cardboard cutout on his arm. "The bathroom's in there. I'll be in in a minute."

A large spa bath dominated the room. It didn't take a genius to work out what he had planned.

"I must have fallen asleep. Not much on tonight." I tried to make light of being caught nana-napping. "I'll be off to bed, then."

Jules took three steps toward me. "I can send her away, you just have to say the word."

I knew if I did there would be no turning back.

He stood in front of me - vulnerable, attractive and available. I realized we'd been dancing around this moment for months.

"I'm sorry. I can't." Lord, I wanted to. I wished I'd never met Nick and gotten myself into a loveless marriage. The best thing that'd ever happened to me was about to climb into a pool of swirling water with God-only-knew-who and it tore at my guts.

He didn't say another word. He turned on his heel and left me alone.

Frustrated and hurt, I buried my head under my pillows, trying to drown out the sounds of laughter and running water.

I closed my eyes and all I could see was a vision of the two of them naked in the water.

Not wanting to see the images in my head, I opened my eyes, still wide awake, all my senses on alert. Listening. Torturing myself.

Why hadn't I gone out with him this evening? Why

couldn't I just cheat on my husband like any other normal, unhappy wife?

A slap. I'd heard a slap. A loud laugh. A strange laugh. The strange laugh of another man. There was another man in the suite. How many people had he brought back?

I snuggled in the warm and comforting softness of the bedclothes. Cold, alone, feeling abandoned.

"Give her another one."

A male voice I didn't know, carrying through the wall from the adjacent bathroom.

"Yes! Again!"

This time the voice was female. A thick accent. How much English did this girl know? Was she one of the throng who'd thrown themselves at Jules this morning?

I felt the stalking fear of nausea. I swallowed, determined I wouldn't be sick.

I started to shake. I wanted to cry. I wanted more than anything to stomp into that bathroom and throw them out.

Instead I tried not to listen. Tried not to hear the sounds of them engaging in what I believed had to be hot and heavy sex. Tried to concentrate on me, on my body, on where I lay.

Listening would mean admitting that the sound of them turned me on. It made me hot to think of Jules. Flashes of him and Sheree on stage came into my mind. Lithe muscles and skin - glistening with a sheen of sweat from the exertion - played across my imagination.

My hands trembled as they ran down my own taut body. Tension pulsed through me. I could feel the wetness of my desire for Jules beginning to pool on the

61

cool sheets beneath me.

I allowed my hands to travel across the warm mountain of my breasts. The tips of my nipples stood, pebble-like under my fingers. Aching for the hot and savage suckle of Jules' mouth. I squeezed each firm nub. Hard. A sharp pain shot through my body, down to the aching, wet swelling below.

Squirming under my own touch, I heard the distinct moan of Jules. Closing my eyes tightly, I saw him before me. His naked chest. I imagined the teasing touch of his chest hair, the scent of him as he lowered his body over my own prostrate form.

My fingers crept ever downward, following the dip and fall of my flat stomach, my heavy, gold belly-button ring seeming to radiate the heat building inside of me. My hands moved from the tender flesh of my belly and followed the steep slope of my hip bones, before my fingers fell to the warm and intimate confines of my swollen cunt.

I caught the sound of another slap, another groan, another growl.

I plunged my fingers inside of myself. Meeting with damp heat, I pleasured myself. My fingers ran over rippled flesh, hunting for my ever evasive g-spot while all the time keeping enough carefully applied pressure on my clit to not quite tip me over the edge.

I strained, listening again for more sounds of Jules. Imagining him here with me now, his hands stealing into me, his mouth on my clit, lapping at my juices, driving me closer and closer to orgasm.

My hands labored over my aroused body, my own slick juices   coating my fingers.   Fingers that brought me steadily closer and closer to climax, working in tandem with a mind intent on creating the perfect fantasy of Jules.

My body began to shudder uncontrollably. I heard a man's orgasmic moan. My breath began to catch in my throat, my chest heaving as my body pulsed beneath my unrelenting fingers. The weight of my fantasy was too much, the echoes of pleasure drifting through the walls and into my consciousness unbearable.

Lost in time, lost in space and lost without Jules, I came, long and hard, with the mournful, murmur of his name on my parched lips.

Exhausted, shuddering, and feeling alone and inadequate, I noticed my iPod sitting on the stark, hotel bedside table. I put the earphones in my ears and set Jules music loud enough so I could drown out the residual moaning from next door.

He sang me into a guilt-ridden, post-orgasmic sleep.

I awoke hours later. The sun streamed in across the fine hotel blind. The usual morning breakfast chatter didn't filter through my door. Tentatively, I ventured out of bed and into the main living area of the suite.

Dan sat reading the morning paper, the remains of his breakfast strewn down one end of the table. "Morning, Mags. You slept well?" The intimation wasn't lost on me.

"No thanks to the party going on next door." I tried to sound as if I didn't care. I doubt I fooled him.

"You're going to get hurt if you hang your heart with him. You know that, don't you?"

I nodded. Dan knew everything that transpired on tour. It would've been useless and silly of me to try and deny my feelings.

"Here. Come and have some breakfast. We can talk about it."

"I'm not hungry and there's nothing to talk about."

He patted the chair next to him. "At least have a cup of coffee before you face the onslaught of the day."

"They got up to no good last night, didn't they?" I allowed Dan to pour me a cup of coffee. It was a waste of time protesting.

"Yes, they did." He replied.

He pushed some fruit and cereal toward me and I moved it aside. I had no appetite at the best of times, which this wasn't. "Why do I feel as if you're Father Dan and I'm Mother Mags?"

Dan laughed at me now. "You're no mother to this lot, Mags. You're feeling like shit this morning because you know what's been going on through that door." He pointed behind him to the large double doors that led to the bedroom where Jules and his God-only-knew-how-many guests spent the night. "And because you and I both know that if you'd have gone out with him last night you'd be the one there in his bed."

"Just fucking stop it. You're being a jerk." I looked down at the steaming brew in front of me. I was even losing my appetite for my beloved coffee.

"He's a virile man, Mags." Dan's voice softened.

"I know that." I felt tears, but refused to surrender to them.

"He doesn't have to apologize for wanting to take what's on offer." He sounded so damn reasonable.

"I know that as well." I thought about my shameful self-pleasure last night. Listening in. I felt like a pervert, a tasteless voyeur of other people's sexual gratification. Unclean. But a small part of me still relished satisfying my own needs in an unconventional way.

"You don't have to be a martyr and be miserable."

I looked up at Dan. "What do you mean?"

"I can tell things aren't as good between you and Nick as you make them out to be."

"Don't start." He had no idea how bad they'd become. I'd been hiding the truth from everyone, including myself.

He held his hand up. "I know you don't want to hear this, Mags, but really, you're not doing yourself or Julian any favors."

"By what?" I snapped at him, my viciousness surprising even me. "I'm supposed to just chuck the husband in who's supported me for years?"

"You support yourself, Mags. He's not supporting you. This entire operation would fall apart if you weren't around."

"I'm not that important."

"Does he tell you that?" Dan had a stern look, a beady-eyed gaze I just knew I couldn't get out from under. I'd seen him in action before. He searched for the truth, mined it like a prospector on the trail of hidden gems. Picking through whatever argument anyone put up until he found the clear, clean gem that held the truth of the matter.

I thought about all the times Nick told me I only had the job because I was a pretty face. That I had no real value, that I was lucky to have him supporting me so I could trot all over the world playing at a job.

"No."

Dan knew I was lying.

He sighed. "Look, love. You're a smart, intelligent, sassy woman. You run this circus like a pro. Christ, you are a pro." He put his hand on top of mine. It was a sweet and fatherly gesture.

I looked up into his eyes and saw concern. Concern for me and for what I was doing with my life.

"We all love you here. We couldn't manage without you. You know I couldn't deal with these reprobates on my own."

"I know." For some reason I just didn't want to feel good about myself this morning. I wanted to crawl back to bed and wish last night hadn't happened. I wanted to wind back the clock and go out with Jules.

"Don't keep putting yourself down, Mags. Don't let anyone tell you that you're not valid. But we've had this discussion before, so how come we're having it again?"

I shrugged. "You're good at seeing the best in people. I mean, you picked up Jules when everyone else had given up on him."

"I saw pain and I saw talent and I saw someone who only needed a chance. Just needed a foot in that crack in the door and I wanted to help him get there."

He squeezed my hand. "I see that in you too, Mags. That's why I wanted you to work with us. That's why I talked Julian into giving you the job. Do you have any idea how many people want to be sitting where you sit day in and day out?"

"Some."

"Well, you're not here for show, or because the main event in there has fallen in love with you."

What little of the coffee I had drunk threatened to make an immediate escape. "I wish you wouldn't say that."

"My dear, Magdeline, I find that speaking the truth puts most things into perspective. I also find that speaking the truth means that those who do not want to deal with their truth eventually have to face it."

Almost as if on cue, the door behind us opened and a disheveled Jules stumbled toward us. And what a lovely truth he was, even semi-comatose after a night of partying. A pair of turquoise boxer shorts hung crookedly off his hips, his hair was mussed and his body bore the scars of frantic sex with strangers. He had bruising around his throat and across his chest, and an assortment of large welts down his sides and over his back.

"What did you have in there - a vampire with talons?" Dan's comments broke the awkward silence.

Jules wouldn't look at me and barely acknowledged my presence. That hurt more than anything else that had happened in the last twenty-four hours.

"Dan." Jules said, "Cut the piss-taking. I need you to get rid of them."

I swirled the coffee in my mug, trying not to look at him, realizing I had no idea what I was feeling. I felt nothing and that scared me.

"I'm not going back in there." Jules turned his attention to me. "Mags, can I use your shower?"

"Use whatever you like, you always do." I looked up at him, straight into those expressive, gorgeous green eyes. "I don't care."

"Thanks."

He slunk off to my bathroom, leaving me to deal with the clean-up and clear-up. He slammed my bedroom door.

Dan looked at me. "Well, you showed him."

"Shut up." I wanted to belt Dan.

"You do care."

"I know that." I wanted to slap them both.

"And so does he."

"Yeah, right. He cares so much you've got a couple of groupies to throw out this morning. You'd better get onto that."

"And you, young lady, had better get in there and sort him out."

"I'll do no such thing. He can stew in his own mess for a while. I'm going out for a walk and he'd better be out of my room when I get back."

"You're not eating. Don't think I haven't noticed that either."

I picked up a muffin off the table, stared Dan down and took a huge bite. I gleaned some delight in dropping the balance back beside my half-drunk cup of coffee.

"Behaving badly does not become you, my dear."

With a mouth full of muffin, I couldn't come back with some pithy retort, so I turned my back on Dan, planning to storm out of the suite.

To my horror, I realized I was still wearing silk pajama trousers and a small yellow singlet. I couldn't traipse through a five-star hotel lobby and out onto the street looking like I'd just been at a slumber party.

I needed to go back into my room if I wanted to leave.

Fuck!

"Not really going anywhere except back in there after him, are you?" Dan sounded suitably smug.

I swallowed the mouthful of muffin and sat back down on the chair, defeated. "Aren't you supposed to be getting rid of the groupies in the bedroom?" At least I didn't have to do that this time. The consolation prize.

"Ah, yes. I'm doing your job this morning."

"Why does everyone just have to be so difficult and argumentative around here?" Poor Dan was wearing my frustration.

"Probably because tempers are flaring." Dan looked at me again; he had a strange knack of making me feel as if he were reading my very thoughts. I wanted to get away from him, but my only place of respite led me straight back to the one person I desperately wanted to avoid.

I could fix the problem. I just wouldn't tour with him anymore.   I couldn't stand the pain of watching him implode. The knowledge of him being with others night after night. The fact that last night there'd been a man in attendance with his usual bimbo disturbed me more than I cared to admit.

I pushed the rest of my breakfast away. If I couldn't control him, at least I could control what went into my mouth and today that would be nothing.

"You can't avoid him all morning. If you want to go walking, you better go in there and get dressed."

"Get out of my head, Dan. I can't cope-"

"When I'm right."

"Okay." Elbows on the table and my eyes hidden from sight, I surrendered. "I'll go in and sort it with him."

"Good girl. I knew you'd see sense in the end." Dan sounded pleased.

Before I could excuse myself from the table, the door to Jules' room opened and two exquisite creatures of the night emerged, trying to remove themselves from the scene of their crimes from the night before. The enchanting and seductive looks that had secured Julian's attentions seemed overdramatic and overdone in the harsh light of morning.

The man resembled a young version of Elvis and wore the battle scars of a night on the town and an early morning of rigorous group sex on his lithe, fit frame. He carried himself with a cockiness that comes from knowing everyone around you finds you attractive. The same attitude Jules oozed when he was on stage, though I now realized that attitude didn't translate into Jules' off-stage life.

To my dismay I found Young Elvis incredibly attractive. If Jules had been with him throughout the night I could certainly understand why.

His cohort could have been any one of the number of blondes who screamed for Jules at the gig last night and I wasn't even sure if she was the same person he'd ushered into the bathroom. They all seemed to blend into one now. I blame *Mattel* - generations of young women brought up with the idea that Barbie was the ideal. Not that Young Elvis - or Jules, for that matter - had any resemblance to Ken.

"Good morning to you," Dan played the respectful host too well, "can we offer you some breakfast."

"Dan," I hissed, "you're supposed to be getting rid of them - not offering them hospitality."

"Trust me, they'll go," he whispered back.

As if on cue, the rest of the band started to trickle in for breakfast, though it could technically be called lunch at this hour of the day. They'd all had a real night out and any plans we had for this morning were likely going to be shelved.

Sheree deposited herself next to me, looking a little less

worse for wear than the Barbie doll fidgeting on the other side of the room. Likely wishing she was somewhere else.

"You missed a great night out." Sheree reached for the fresh, steaming coffeepot Frederick had set down on the table in front of us.

"I can see that," I said. "The carnage from Jules' room was trying to make a quiet exit before you lot arrived."

She shuddered. "Ugh. I'd hate to be them. Poor things, running the gauntlet of this mob." Sheree didn't try to keep her voice down, causing Barbie to squirm some more.

Breakfast appeared to be degenerating into a scrum for hangover cures. I'd not been part of the night before, so didn't want a starring role in the morning after. As much as I loathed the thought of retreating to my room, it was beginning to seem far more palatable than the zoo scene playing out before me.

Barbie, looking more uncomfortable than ever, scanned the room, no doubt trying to find Jules.

I couldn't help myself. "He's shot through. Probably won't resurface again until we're leaving."

I didn't feel any guilt for the cutting comments, even when a forlorn and lost look appeared on her perfect features. The Universe, I knew, would repay me handsomely for my small moment of evil satisfaction.

Barbie groped wildly for the hand of Young Elvis. Could they be a couple? From the self-conscious way they touched, probably not. But, abandoned by the focus of her desires and with her senses assaulted by the circus that is the band the morning after, I suppose Young Elvis became her life raft in a sea of insanity.

Stiffly they made their way toward the door.

71

Young Elvis spoke, his voice a singsong of light melody. "I think we should be getting on our way." He started to negotiate his way through the band, Barbie close behind. They didn't have a chance of making a fast exit. The band liked to torment overnighters, the way a cat plays with a mouse.

I decided, they weren't a couple. Their body language spoke of two people – well, three if you included Jules - who'd come together for a night and now in the harsh light of morning had nothing in common except a shared past of a few awkward and exhilarating hours.

I didn't know how anyone could do one-night stands. I saw them over and over when we were on tour. Another city, another man or woman, constant moving on. It was something I'd never been able to do. In that respect I suppose I was different from the band I traveled with. They had appetites and they allowed themselves to meet them. I had to concede, it must be hard to say "no" when after each show the entire city seemed to be on offer like some sort of homo sapiens smorgasbord.

Sheree poked me in the arm. "He's obviously not batting for the other side then?"

"What are you talking about?"

"Last night the boys couldn't decide if he was gay." Sheree slurped her coffee and bit into another muffin, crumbs cascading down onto the table and sitting like miniature chunks of coal on the silver knife-and-spoon setting. The slovenly demeanor of the morning grated my nerves. I'd become part of a chimps' tea party.

"And so they sent him home with Jules?" I didn't understand. Jules never picked up his own partners - there were too many eager women waiting for him. He took a look, chose someone and then had Otis or Verne escort a girl back to the suite.

"Nah. Julian wanted her, but the guy seemed to be part of a package deal."

Strange, I thought. Jules didn't often have other men back. "Did Jules think he was gay?"

"Don't think so." Sheree spoke through a mouthful of breakfast. "He just liked the look of the guy too."

My heartbeat quickened. "Were there any press about? You know what they're like."

"Publicity likes the speculation about his sexuality - you know that."

I did know that. But what publicity didn't know was that Nick was homophobic. Anything that resembled more than speculation about Jules' sexuality would have him arriving on the first plane demanding I exit the tour.

The thought terrified me.

"I know, but was there any press there?" I continued to badger Sheree.

She shrugged. "Who knows? We were all past caring by then."

"So nobody saw them come up here?"

"Doubt it. But the hordes will be down below trying to buy a story."

Time for action. "Hang on you two!" The entire crew at breakfast, together with Young Elvis and Barbie, stared at me.

"Dan," I hissed, "get hold of Otis or Verne - now."

"What's the deal, Mags?" Dan looked at me as if I'd lost my mind.

"Escort the two of them out the back entrance. I don't want the press getting hold of the fact he spent the night with Jules."

"Publicity will hate you."

"Fuck publicity. This is about me for a change."

As much as I didn't particularly want to go anywhere near our overnight guests, I covered the short distance to the other side of the room in a moment. Making sure I was between them and the exit.

"Hi. I know you guys don't want to stay." I felt awkward, as if I were the one who'd just woken up in someone else's place. "But there's likely to be a rugby scrum of press downstairs."

Barbie went white under what was left of her smeared foundation.

"I'm sure you don't want to be molested by photographers and hack journalists, so we're going to arrange for a taxi to come and pick you up from around the back. It'll take you anywhere you want to go. At our expense."

Barbie looked relieved. Young Elvis I couldn't read and that set off my internal alarm system. I was good at reading people and this man, who'd spent an intimate evening with Jules, seemed rather untouched and untouchable.

"Thank you. So much." Barbie's over-exuberant gratitude pained me. I could only assume English was her second language, her words blanketed in a thick accent of European descent. Although it occurred to me Jules wouldn't have been worried about her linguistic skills last night, no doubt more interested in a number of other things she could do with her collagen-filled lips.

"Is there somewhere else we can wait?" It was Young Elvis' turn to shuffle in an uncomfortable way near the door - presumably because Ted was blowing kisses at him across the room and making all manner of strong-arm sexual gestures. Ted exceled at making people feel uncomfortable the *morning-after-the-night-before*. It was his touring trademark.

I almost felt sorry for them both. But then I remembered how vile it had been listening to them going at it for most of the night.

"Just give me a moment. I won't be long." I went back to the breakfast brawl on the other side of the room. "Can't you jerks behave for a minute?"

Ted smiled his most dazzling smile. Frederick took over where he'd left off, only this time he made lewd noises. It was almost as if he'd been here last night too. I shuddered.

"Will you two just knock it off?" I looked to Dan for support. He pulled a face and raised his shoulders in a *what-do-you-think-I-can-do* gesture. "Is anyone in touch with Otis? It's not as if I can go out there looking like this to hunt him down."

"Isn't he usually parked outside the door?" Sheree said as she wiped muffin crumbs off her face.

"Of course he is. Why isn't he in here yet?" I made for the entranceway.

"Just calm down, Mags." Dan had obviously decided to come to my rescue. "Go and get yourself decent. I'll deal with this." He pulled me aside, making it look as if we were involved in some sort of conspiracy. "You've got enough to worry about in there." He cast his head toward my door.

"How could I forget?" Caught between the insanity of having to shuffle Jules' early morning entertainment out of the door unnoticed and facing him, Jules had become the more desirable option. "Just make sure they get out of here without selling their souls to the tabloids, would you?"

"You know you can count on me, Mags. Now go and sort out your relationship with our star, or I fear the tour is going to dissolve before we make the Pacific."

"And then you'll never get to tick whale watching off your list of things to do before you die."

"Exactly."

As I made my way toward my room and Jules I could hear Dan casting orders about. I figured he'd have to organize it all. I had a very large whale to fry.

CHAPTER SEVEN

I sat on my bed, curled in a little ball of resentment, pissed off that he was still in my bathroom. Unable to walk in there and scream and yell and rant and rave, which I wanted to do. How dare he treat me like this? How dare he have that man and that woman and then come here, into my private space and flaunt himself in front of me?

As if on cue, I heard the water stop. The door opened and he stood still, the last swirls of steam escaping around him. He looked as he often did on stage, with the bright light and mist coming from behind him.

Almost godlike.

The vision of him blew my mind. I was in love and there wasn't a thing I could do about that.

I wanted him and there wasn't a damn thing I could do about that either.

He knew he'd crossed a line, and yet here he stood.

All arrogance and desire.

Wrapped at the waist in a white hotel towel, small droplets of water running down his chest, navigating their way through the forest of chest hair.

I wanted him.

I wanted to lick him dry.

I wanted to trace the path of those droplets with my tongue.

He walked toward me, saying not a single word.

His warm, wet and soap-smelling torso touched mine. His probing tongue found my waiting mouth. Humid, clean heat emanated from his tense body.

Leaning over me, he shook, the sculptured muscles of his arms and shoulders standing proud from the bulk of his frame. I felt myself respond, my chest lifting to be closer to him. I wanted him and I had no control. Need and desire washed away my fury. My body resonated with the silent call of his.

"I want you so much." The words sounded foreign to me, even as they fell from my lips.

"I know." He whispered back around our tongues.

There was an urgent knocking on the door. "Mags!"

"For fuck's sake!" Jules exploded.

The moment was lost.

He flung the door open - the force enough, I thought, to tear it from its hinges. "What!"

Peering around his semi-naked body, I could see the entire crew looking dumbstruck at us.

"Julian, man. Chill." Frederick looked as if he'd been eating hash cookies for breakfast, his eyes rotating in opposite directions in his head. "Dan's sorting the couple you jumped last night but the hotel transport people say there's a problem with the account. He needs Mags."

"Everyone always needs fucking Mags." Jules cast a despairing glance back toward me. "That's half the problem around here."

Frederick wrung his hands, dancing on the spot in front of Julian. "Sorry, man, but there's nothing I can do - he asked for her."

Jules sighed, resigned to our respective fates. "Don't worry, pal. She'll get it sorted. Won't you, Mags?" A stupefied Frederick registered the sentence, his eyes seeming to still for a moment.

"Yes. I always do." I muttered.

Jules pushed past Frederick, I could only assume on his way to his room.

"Tell Dan I'll be there in a minute and shut the door," I said, "I need to get dressed before I can go down there."

Frederick pulled the door closed. Alone and with a sense of great heaviness, I lifted myself up off the bed.

What would have happened if we hadn't been interrupted? What would I have been doing right this very second? A sense of grief overwhelmed me.

For me, for Nick or for Jules – who knew?

My worst nightmare. The papers lay across the tables in the bus, their headlines taunting me.

Young Elvis had gone to the press in the worst possible way. *Julian – Out of the Closet and Into My Arms,* the headline read. Not a mention of Barbie anywhere. The scoop read as if Jules had been disguising his sexuality but now that Young Elvis had come into his life love had blossomed and all could be revealed. My heart sank.

"I wonder if this is how George Michael's manager felt?" Dan despaired. "The record company's been on the phone already wanting to know what the hell's going on."

Jules, torn between mortification and an insane sense of pride, had hidden himself in his room upstairs.

"You did a great job of keeping the lid on that." I threw another trashy tabloid across the bus at Dan.

Julian's Slapper Seconds, the lurid headline read over airbrushed photos of a perfectly coiffured Barbie and Young Elvis. I got as far as reading Young Elvis' account of his sensational lovemaking with Jules and put the paper down. I wanted to be sick.

Dan said, "We should be grateful that at least the stories conflict with each other."

"We should?" I found it difficult to be grateful for anything at the moment.

"Who the hell found them and why weren't the stories shut down?" I thought about Young Elvis. Had he planned to take this to the media from the outset?

Dan interrupted my pondering. "Publicity-"

"Don't start with the publicity shit. This does him far more damage than good." I was furious. "If the label has been on the phone to you already it's not good for publicity."

"Sales." Dan's monotone infuriated me even more, even if he did sound as despondent as I felt.

"This prick is suggesting Jules is gay, for crying out loud. How the hell can that be good for record sales?"

And forget record sales, the thought of that man with Jules did something to me. It twisted my feelings in a way I didn't understand. I'd expected to feel jealousy and revulsion; instead the image of them together created a deep, animal longing. Every time I closed my eyes, all I could see was their entwined bodies. I smelt the acrid scent of heated man, heard the sounds of rough, male lovemaking.

I shook my head. Focused my attention on Dan.

"Publicity's been on the phone - sales are soaring every house is full. They just can't get enough of him. He's a gay icon," Dan despaired.

"Gay icon, my arse!"

"It's his arse they're after, love."

"Don't go there either!" Why couldn't I get them to see how dangerous this was for me? "Do you have any idea how Nick will react if he sees this shit?"

"Mags, nobody's going to care."

"I care and Nick will have a mental breakdown. Has it made the internet? What bloody chance have we got of containing this?"

"We've got no control, you know that." Dan stood over me and scratched his head. No doubt exasperated with my moaning and ranting. "It's not like I'm throwing this stuff out there."

"The record company might be?" I hated them, they drove us on tour. "I wouldn't put it past them."

"Mags, you know I won't allow the man to be crucified, just to make money."

I knew Dan; he wouldn't do that to Jules. He loved him, probably more than I did. I flipped open the lid of my laptop, compelled by a sense of indignation and urgency, willing the hard drive to whirr into action sooner.

Dan sat down next to me. The bulk of his large frame, flabby from too many self-indulgent nights touring, trapped me in the small space.

I needed to escape, to explode - to do something to control this uncontrollable nightmare. Dan grabbed my hands, preventing me from googling the latest news stories on Jules.

"Stop doing this. You're going to drive yourself to a

nervous breakdown."

"But, Nick - "

"Fuck, Nick!"

The sudden explosion from Dan shook me. "Weren't you listening to a word I said yesterday morning?" No one understood.

"Calm down, would you?" Dan forced me to be still and look at him.

I was aware that Sheree, Frederick and Ted, though feigning reading the tabloids, also had one ear tuned into our conversation. Nothing was sacred on tour. I didn't need them gossiping about the state of my marriage or about me and Jules.

"You think they don't know what's been going on?" Dan wouldn't let my hands go. He forced me to keep my attention on him.

I thought of Sheree and her difficulties. I didn't want her to witness the demolition of my marriage.

"I know those two do." I motioned to Verne and Otis who sat quietly at the bottom of the circular staircase. "I don't expect everyone else knows all my business."

"You and Jules have been the last two to work it out."

"Sheree doesn't know," I said, thinking about our conversation earlier during the week.

"She's too wrapped up in her own problems. Everyone else has a handle on what's going on." Dan let go my hands to wipe his brow. "So you can just calm down."

That gave me the split second I needed to press the enter button. A page of search reports on Jules and Young Elvis filled the small screen.

My stomach lurched in response.

"I can't calm down. I don't want everyone involved in

the implosion of my marriage and I especially don't want a scene with Nick here because of some idiotic tabloid newspapers or crap reporting on the internet."

I dropped my head into my hands. There was simply no way Nick wouldn't know what was going on.

I flipped the computer around so Dan could see. "I'm sunk."

"No, you're not. We have two more nights and then we're on our way to the Pacific for our planned break. You can sort it out before we go on the second leg."

"If I make it to the second leg. There's an email from him here."

"What does he say?"

"He trusts that I can confirm that the rumor-mill and the second-rate hacks who dominate the daily papers are on the wrong track and that we've leaked the story ourselves to boost sales."

"Bingo! He's let you off the hook. Brilliant strategy. Just tell him he's right. It'll all die down in a couple of days and he'll be none the wiser."

"You make it seem so simple."

He hugged me, and then kissed me on the top of the head. "That's because, my darling, it is."

Dan left me to compose an email to Nick. There was too much going through my head.

How did I feel about lying?

I hated lying.

Loathed it, in fact.

So had I been lying to myself for a long time about Jules? What really happened with Young Elvis? Did I care? Did it change the way I felt about Jules? And how the hell was I going to cope with Nick now?

I couldn't reply to him properly yet. I needed time to think - time to process and time to work out what I wanted. The next few days away would surely consolidate my thoughts and feelings?

Meanwhile I sent Nick a single sentence. "Total crap – daily hack-feeding frenzy!"

No lies and no deceit.

Yeah, right.

There may have been no lies or deceit, but Nick saw straight through the evasive email and caught the next flight out of Dubai. He arrived at the door of the suite before I knew what the hell was going on.

"I don't give a shit about who he is or how fucking wonderful the rest of the world believe him to be. You're my wife and you're not sticking around so some of the shit the tabloids are throwing about can stick to you!"

I noticed the veins on the side of his neck were sticking out. "You can't just fly yourself in here and demand that I chuck in a career I love."

"This! A career?" He laughed - the kind of laugh that made me want to smash the cut-crystal jug I was holding into the side of his head.

"What the fuck do you know about what I do here?"

He threw the paper he'd been brandishing at me across the room. "Enough that the directors and shareholders of the Boards I sit on can see that he's a pervert and my wife works for him."

"I don't work for him." I gritted my teeth. "I work *with* him."

"With him, for him. It's semantics." Nick pulled my traveling case out of the wardrobe. "You're leaving – right now."

"You can just put that back where you got it from. I'm not going anywhere."

"Don't argue." Nick flung the bag on the bed and started tipping the contents of my drawers into the case. "You're leaving and that's all there is to it."

As fast as he tipped the meager contents of my traveling wardrobe into my case, I unpacked it and put it back in the drawers.

"I. Am. Not. Going. Anywhere." I repeated the words through gritted teeth.

Clothing made several runs from the bed to the drawer and back again before Nick stopped in his tracks. "I am not leaving you here."

"And I'm not going anywhere. I'm on tour and I'm staying on tour."

The room looked as if a troop of gypsies had been through. Shirts, underwear and jeans lay in a trail between the bed, the case and the small dresser.

Nick said, "I don't think you understand the severity of the situation, or the impact this is having on my business interests."

"I don't give a flying fuck about your business interests." *Or our marriage.* The words sat unsaid on my tongue, tantalizingly close to escape. Not now. Not the way he'd been behaving. It had all become quite clear to me.

Exhausted, Nick sat down on the edge of the bed. "At least you're still sleeping alone." He flicked his head toward the crisp and unruffled side of the king-size bed, its clean lines in stark contrast to the crumpled side I slept on.

I'd tossed and turned most of the night, unable to stop fantasizing about where the kiss Jules and I had stolen would have gone if we'd not been interrupted. Sleep had come at almost dawn and my dreams were filled with images of a naked and thrusting Young Elvis. I was exhausted and didn't need Nick's third-Reich interrogation, or his bullying insistence that I should leave.

Feeling as if he'd been reading my mind, I snapped, "And what's that supposed to mean?"

"Well, there seems to be a complete lack of morals about this whole business."

Nick had never approved of touring. I began to see him for the narrow-minded snob he really was. "And now you're suggesting I don't have any either."

"You said it." He looked smug. "Not me."

There was a hammering at the door.

"Whoever it is, tell them to go away." He crossed his legs, the perfect creases of his business suit looking as if they could cut him in half.

"I will do no such thing." I couldn't hide my irritation. Everything about him irritated me. "I don't know who the hell you think you are, arriving here unannounced and trying to throw your weight around."

"I think I am your husband, but you seem to have forgotten that fact."

The last thing I could have forgotten at the present time was that I was married. I chose to ignore his further baiting and opened the door.

Dan burst in the room, taking no notice of the fact that a small tornado in the form of Nick had been through the place. He also completely disregarded Nick.

"Where's Julian?"

"I have no idea." Dan was clearly frantic. "What's the matter?"

86

"The label has dumped us." He cast his eyes around the room, like a hunter looking for wary prey.

"What! What do you mean?"

"You heard me. Dumped."

"Why?" I asked.

Nick said sarcastically, "Why do you think?"

"Oh, hello, Nick. When did you get here?" Dan looked about as pleased to see Nick as a rabbit would be after running into a weasel in its burrow.

"This morning. I read those appalling reports on the net and booked the first available flight."

"Yes, well..." Dan scratched his head, fixing me in his gaze, under lowered lashes. "You shouldn't believe all the crap the tabloids are so happy to report."

"The record company obviously does. They appear to be cutting and running."

I could have belted Nick for his supercilious attitude. "Does Jules know?" Nick could crawl back to whatever Middle Eastern hole he'd crawled out of as far as I was concerned. I feared Jules would take this badly and I wanted to be there for him.

"I can't find him. I thought you might know where he is."

Nick asked smugly, "Have you checked with his new boyfriend?"

Before I could react, Dan crossed the room and punched Nick square in the nose. Blood poured down his face, leaving a trail of crimson across his neat and prim white shirt. Nick's blue eyes, almost hidden behind his cupped hands were wide with shock and fear.

"For crying out loud, Dan." I fled to the adjoining bathroom to find a hand towel, more concerned for the hotel carpet than for Nick's nose.

"He fucking deserved it, the little cunt." Dan yelled through the bathroom door. "If you see Julian, can you let him know I need to speak to him?"

I emerged from the bathroom in time to catch the first drip of blood as it made its escape from Nick's hands, which remained clutched to his nose.

"And-" Dan eyeballed Nick before he left the room "-if I find out that anyone has got to Julian before I have and told him what's going on, they'll have more than a sore fucking nose to worry about."

Nick's bloodied hands grasped for the cool, damp towel, holding it to his gushing nostrils. Not a sound came from behind the now crimson toweling.

"He won't hear anything from us." I looked at Nick, who nodded in agreement. "But let me know when you've told him, won't you?"

"I will." Dan turned his full attention back to me. "Come find me when you've got a minute. We need to talk."

I knew he meant when Nick wasn't around. From the look on his bloodied face, Nick did too.

CHAPTER EIGHT

I'd dragged Nick into the bathroom to clean him up.

"They're all animals. The lot of them. The sooner you're out of here the better." Nick inspected the bruise developing around the bridge of his nose. It didn't complement the shade of his skin, but in a strange way it brought out the blue of his eyes.

Jules and Nick were polar opposites, the complete antithesis of each other. Nick's willowy, boyish physique could have something to do with his aversion to homosexuality. Perhaps he'd been preyed upon one too many times at boarding school.

"You just refuse to listen to me. As always." I said. For our entire marriage, it had been like talking to a slab of ice.

"I don't listen because you simply cannot make any kind of a sensible decision for yourself." Nick made another assessment of the state of his nose, wincing as he probed the area with his index finger. "They're just animals, plain and simple. Animals."

"They are not animals and I wish you'd stop saying

that."

"Have you seen the state of my face?" He spun around from the mirror, gesticulating wildly at the kaleidoscope of color that had become his nose.

I felt like telling him a near blind man couldn't miss it, but I kept quiet, preventing the words from escaping my tongue like tiny guided missiles.

Instead I sighed. "I'm not leaving the tour, Nick."

He opened his mouth to say something, thought better of it, and in place of unsaid words just looked through me. I always felt as if I didn't really exist in his world. Now I knew that to be our truth.

He turned his back on me then. In a moment there was more distance between us in this little room than there'd ever been when he was on the other side of the world.

"I'll be taking the next flight out of here." His words were clipped. But after years of marriage I knew their meaning. I'd heard him dispense with many a business partner before they even realized they were on the way out. His colleagues called him the smiling assassin for that very reason.

He had just used the same tone with me.

He added, "You'd best take your animal tour-manager's advice and go look for your darling Julian."

"He's not my darling." A useless denial.

"It's been clear to me for years that he wants to be and you've just made your choice." He turned around again and I saw the pain of resolution and rejection in his eyes. "I won't get in your way." He dabbed at his swollen nose again, wincing in pain.

"Let me help." I made to get a new towel for him, but

he held his hand up, not allowing me within his own small, sacred space.

"You've done enough. I don't want your kind of help anymore. Go find your rock star."

I found Jules sitting in front of the wide-screen TV - another nature documentary, the plight of the Tibetan elk - his face blank and expressionless.

"Did Dan find you?"

"Yes."

"How are you doing?"

"Fine." He didn't sound fine.

"Fucked up, insecure, neurotic and emotional."

"I don't need your self-help analysis at the moment. I thought you were with your husband."

If his words were intended to hurt me, they did.

"He's leaving." And he's leaving me, I wanted to say, but I didn't think Jules wanted to hear.

"I suppose you're going with him now I've been dropped. Everyone else can just pack the fuck up and get out of here as well."

"No one's leaving you, Jules." Least of all me, I thought.

"Press got hold of this yet, have they?"

"I don't know. I'll check the internet if you want."

He shrugged. "Do what you like." Now he was starting to sound like Nick. A sudden feeling of abandonment came over me.

He was more focused on the images of slaughtered elk on the screen in front of him than on me or the problem at hand. I wanted to shake him. Belt him, like Nick had been belted. I'd never seen him so unemotional and

91

vague.

"You want me to find Dan? Or Frederick or Ted?" He shouldn't be sitting here by himself and he clearly didn't want me around.

He shrugged again.

Helplessness added itself to the maelstrom of emotions flooding through me.

I sat down next to him. His lack of animation and eerie disconnectedness scared me. I took his hand in mine, the touch not seeming to even register. His fingers felt like cool porcelain.

I decided he must be in some kind of mild shock.

"Do you know where Dan is?" My words were soft and gentle; it felt as if I were talking to an invalid, not my darling, exuberant Jules.

"No."

"I'm going to find him. You stay here." Not that I thought for a moment Jules would go anywhere. His eyes had never moved from the depressing images of elk being hunted on the Tibetan plains.

I left the room, feeling the need to close the large, heavy door with some care. I feared any loud noise would send Jules over the edge - or was I protecting my nerves?

The outer part of the suite seemed disconcertingly quiet; the usual milling bodies had evaporated. The entire complex of rooms had an air of death about them. It was as if Jules had died and the entire tour team had gone into mourning. I shuddered.

"Get a grip on yourself." Speaking the words aloud brought my organizing mind into focus.

Work. There was work to be done here. We needed a strategy.

I put my misgivings about my current marital status on hold. I needed to find the boys. On a mission, I located Verne just outside the door of the suite.

"Do you have any idea where everyone is?"

He shrugged. "Most of them are in their rooms, I think. I've never seen it so quiet."

I nodded. "I know what you mean." I cast a small smile in his direction. "Well, Verne, my man, that's all about to change."

"You about to round them all up?"

"That I am. Can you put the word about for me?" I knew he was still wirelessly attached to Otis.

"You go back in there and sort out his nibs. Leave it to me. You'll have a full house in about twenty minutes."

"Good man. I knew I could count on you." What Verne didn't know about the whereabouts of the band wasn't worth knowing. I had a second thought. "I don't want everyone, Verne."

"Just your tight eight?"

I nodded. "Just the tight eight." I turned and re-entered our suite, satisfied I could do something toward pulling us all back from the brink.

Nick emerged from my room, his compact, exquisite travel satchel in hand. I stopped. "You're going then?"

"Of course I'm going."

I felt the world do a slight tilt to the left. This is what needed to happen, but I hadn't anticipated the overwhelming sense of panic that assaulted me. We'd argued so many times about my working with Jules, I'd half expected him to calm down and help me manage the situation.

"I'm not sticking around here with these clods." Nick

unconsciously touched his nose again.

I flinched. "Nick, you know things are just a little tense here at the moment."

"All the more reason for me to be on my way. You've made it perfectly clear where your loyalties lie."

He went to walk past me and then must have thought the better of it. "Look." He was no more than a few inches from me now, but he may as well have been on the other side of the room for the lack of intimacy I felt between us. "I want you out of here, I've always wanted you out of here and yet you insist on staying. Our marriage is over as far as I'm concerned."

He stared me down over his bruised and swollen nose, almost challenging me to prove him wrong. "You've got impending disaster to try and avert, then you're taking this tribe of idiots on a ten-day drinking and drugging binge in the Pacific. I want no part of that?"

"You always meet us on the break between legs." If he didn't the entire tour would know my marriage was over. I felt strangely hurt, and also realized after the words were out of my mouth that I sounded pathetic.

"That was before Muhammad Ali back there decided to break my nose."

"But - "

"But fucking nothing. Go away with your perverts, bullies and drug addicts, I won't be there when you get back."

I stood there like a possum in headlights as he walked out of the suite and my life.

I couldn't move. Rooted to the spot wondering what to do now. My sense of aloneness was intensified by the stark, hotel interior. I realized for a moment I wasn't even sure which town we were in. They all looked the same. My life had become that of a gypsy, trailing from one upmarket hotel suite to another. I could be in the middle of Russia or on the central plains of Africa. One city, one hotel suite. The nearest thing I had to stability and a sense of self had just walked out the door.

My skin prickled, my head swam and a familiar stream of nausea overcame me.

I slumped down into one of the leather sofas adorning the room, allowing myself to feel the emotions. If I absorbed them, let them wash over me, then maybe I could cope. I stifled a deep-seated urge to scream, or throw a tantrum like a two-year-old. It was all going wrong. I felt as if my world was slipping away from me.

The room exploded in a chorus of noise and I opened my eyes to see Otis had done his job and rounded up the required troops. Not having a chance to wallow in my own fear and doubt was a good thing, I decided.

"Otis said you wanted to talk to us all." Frederick stated the obvious, as was Frederick's way.

I quickly scanned the room and noted someone was missing. "Where's Dan?"

"He shouldn't be too far away." Sheree eyed me with concern. "Someone said Nick was here."

I could tell by the look on her face Dan must have told her what happened. "He had to go."

"But Jeremy was looking forward to catching up with him."

I'd forgotten Jeremy was coming on our short sabbatical. I waved my hand dismissively. "There'll be another time."

"Will there? It's just Jeremy's arriving in a couple of

days and I'll have to explain to him why Nick's not here." Sheree's tone was almost accusatory.

"Of course I'm sure. What kind of a stupid question is that?" I didn't try to hide my irritation with her cross-examination.

"Well, I don't know. I just heard -"

"You shouldn't believe everything you hear. Sometimes people get it wrong." My words had temporarily cut her off but I needed some kind of immediate distraction from where this conversation was heading. Where the hell was Dan?

The ever-lovely Frederick came to my rescue. "Have you seen Julian this morning, Mags?"

Many people painted Frederick as a musical bum - a genius musical bum, but still a bum. He modeled himself on Keith Richards of the Rolling Stones, only his face didn't yet have the leathery, worn-out edge enjoyed by Keith.

"I have," I said. "Have any of you spent any time with him today?

Heads shook in unison. The assembled crowd reminded me of a line of open-mouthed clowns.

"Shame on the lot of you. He needs us." Although why I thought anyone else could comfort the morbid, staring creature I'd left in front of the wide-screen plasma TV seemed beyond me.

"You know what he's like," Sheree piped up. "He'd rather wrestle a python on stage than be with anyone when he's down."

"He wouldn't wrestle it, he'd give it the kiss of life. And besides-" Frederick winked at me "-that's what he has you around for."

The crew erupted into a fit of cackling laughter.

"Just shut up." I enjoyed a moment's respite from the air of tension encompassing us.

Dan joined the troupe, looking tired. He always wore stress like a cumbersome robe.

"I'm glad you've got everyone together, Mags." He ran his fingers through his hair, reminding me of a crazed professor. "Now I'm presuming the jungle drums have beaten well and you've all heard that the label has dropped us?"

A collective moan of disapproval. Now the nodding heads reminded me of the toy tigers that used to sit on the dashboard of my grandfather's car.

"Bastards. What's it all about, Dan?" Frederick's usual casual demeanor had been replaced by one of open aggression.

Dan cast me a fleeting glance, conveying his despair and urging me to answer the difficult question.

"It doesn't really matter what it's about." I took the floor for him.

"That shit about him being gay's done it, hasn't it?" Sheree voiced the thought that had been going through most of our minds.

"But that's just so seventies." Frederick couldn't hide his disgust. "Those idiots who live in ivory towers and always have to placate the shareholders." He was on his personal soapbox now. "Who go to church on Sundays to redeem themselves after a week of raping, pillaging, and coveting each other's wives. They need a right kick up the ass."

"Have you finished your redneck ranting, Fred?" Dan tried to secure a hold over the quickly degenerating conversation.

97

"You know what I mean, Dan." Frederick's face, usually smooth, carefree and serene had taken on the tone of a ravaged landscape. Blue veins stuck out of the side of his neck like swollen rivers. He looked more like Keith Richards by the second.

"I do, I do. We don't need to get up in arms about it."

I tried to intervene. "But - "

Now Dan cut me off, holding up his hands for silence, trying to quell the growing emotions. "Mags, troops, we need to not go off half-cocked here."

"Isn't that the problem? What he's been up to with his cock?" Sheree's uncharacteristic outburst took me by surprise.

Suppressed laughter came from somewhere in the group.

"What he's supposedly been up to." Frederick raced to the defense of his creative partner.

"Sorry." Dan blushed, which was unusual for him. "Bad choice of words."

"It's not your bad choices that have got us in this mess." Sheree again. "Our livelihoods are at stake and he won't even come out here and talk to us."

"I don't know what you're worrying about; your husband would be delighted if you weren't on the road anymore." Frederick couldn't contain his frustration.

"Just leave Jeremy out of this."

"Why should I? He sits there with a moronic look of doom and despair on his face every time we're heading off on a tour."

The door opened and Jules, no longer zombie-like, stepped into the fracas.

"What's all the fucking noise about? A man gets

dropped by his label, wants to sit there and sulk in quiet and all I can hear is you lot behaving badly."

All assembled fell silent, like students up before the headmaster after doing something appalling to bring the school's reputation into disrepute.

"Sorry, Jules." I felt an instant need to resolve the issues. "We were just having a meeting." And to explain. "We wanted to work out what we could do to make things better for you."

"Yeah, mate. It's just a lousy thing." Frederick gave Jules a bear hug.

A lump formed in my throat.

"Come here, the lot of you." Jules held his arms out and we formed the tight circle we adopted before each show.

He started the pre-show mantra and each of us responded in turn. The rhythmic and prayer-like chanting easing and settling our nervousness.

How did he do that? How did he take a bunch of quarreling followers and settle us?

A sense of unity, a sense of we-can-get-through-this, a sense of all-will-be-okay now pervaded the room. A single, humble gesture from the man who should rightly have been incensed by his record label's disloyalty brought us all back from the fringe. Tears prickled at my eyes and I wished I could blame it on hay fever.

"Now." Jules straightened up. Disengaged himself from us and took control. Center stage, where he was comfortable and where he belonged.

"Since when have we let a few pathetic headlines in garbage dailies cause us a problem?"

There was a murmur of *Never*.

"And since when have we ever worried about what those idiots at the label think about me?"

"We haven't." I could see Frederick relaxing right before my very eyes.

Jules ran his fingers through his dark hair. I thought I saw a glint of gray over his temple.

Dan pointed out, "They haven't dropped you before."

I threw Dan a warning stare, but he held his ground.

Jules turned to face him, intense green eyes flashing. "We don't need them, Danny boy. They need me."

"That's right. It's their loss." Ted, ever loyal Ted. "We've still got bums on seats and a tour to finish."

Dan frowned back at Jules. "You seriously want to use this, to keep bums on seats?"

"Don't see why we shouldn't. What are we paying that PR crowd for if they can't put some kind of spin on this?"

Dan looked to me. "Mags, we need you to get hold of them. See what they can do to capitalize on this."

I nodded.

"We're off for some R and R soon. See what local charity you can get me involved in where we're going." Jules was thinking outside the square.

"It's worse than being in politics." Sheree looked appalled. Do you think this is how they all stood around in the oval office after the Monika Lewinsky story broke?"

I nodded. "I'm sure they did."

Jules put his arm around me. A shot of pure electricity raced through my side. He pulled Dan close to the other side of him. Jules remained, sandwiched between the two of us.

"Bill Clinton didn't have the top team at his disposal that I've got."

A rush of pride and excitement prickled my skin; I felt the warmth of a blush escaping my cheeks.

We were a top team and this was where I belonged. With my dysfunctional, touring family. Nick was right; he wasn't a part of this and he never would be. For me, it was simply life itself.

Jules broke from Dan, but held me firm at his side.

"Can you get onto the PR people, Dan?" Jules gave me a squeeze. I liked it. "I know it's usually Mags' area of expertise, but I want to talk to her and we need to contain damage as soon as we can on this one."

"No problems." Dan gave me a knowing glance before leaving the room.

The rest of the troops had settled themselves into the outer room of the suite. They knew it was imperative at a time like this they stayed and showed solidarity as a group. Otis had taken up his position by the inside of the main door; Verne was no doubt already outside. Sheree and Ted were settling down to play cards and Fred had picked up a guitar and started to tune it.

Jules ran his hand lightly across the small of my back, before picking up my hand in his and leading me into the room next door. His bedroom.

CHAPTER NINE

"Close the door."

Mesmerized by the sound of the words, I simply did as I was told.

My hand had barely left the cool copper of the handle before Jules had circumnavigated my body and I was brought back to my senses by the loud click of the lock as he made sure we had privacy.

I looked up at him. "You never lock the door."

"I'm going to be changing a lot of things from now on."

He sat back on the bed, where not more than an hour ago he'd watched elk being slaughtered. Picking up the remote control, he hit the mute button. Silent images of snakes danced their way across the hot and dusty Australian desert.

"You know I love you, don't you, Mags?"

I nodded. "Everyone else knows that too, according to Dan."

"There's not a lot gets past our crew."

"I guess that's what happens when you all live on a bus for weeks on end." I shuffled nervously in front of the locked bedroom door, noticing the hotel staff hadn't vacuumed carefully around the doorstop. A thick layer of carpet fluff had accumulated beneath the wide brass rod.

"Is Nick still here?"

"No. He's gone."

I tore my eyes from the floor, catching an intense look from Jules which registered deep in my stomach. Then I thought to ask, "How did you know he was here?"

"Otis told me. He said Dan had clobbered him one."

"He did."

"Why?"

"Because Nick's homophobic and was making disparaging comments about you."

"So Dan the man decided he had to defend my honor." Jules grinned.

"Something like that."

"Otis told me that you and Nick were fighting." His voice remained cool and calm. It almost sounded as if he were singing me a lullaby, not interrogating me on the current state of my marriage.

"Is there anything Otis doesn't tell you?"

"He doesn't tell me who he's fucking."

"And neither should he."

"But he tells me who everyone else is fucking."

"Is that right?" The tone of our conversation had changed.

"It is." He patted the bed beside him. "Come sit with me."

I moved toward Jules, tired of trying to resist the attraction. "So if I asked Otis, would he tell me who you've been fucking on the tour?" I sat down next to him. No more than a couple of inches separating us. Dingo the same color as the Australian desert ran at full speed across the quiet plasma screen before us.

"You don't have to ask Otis - I'll tell you if you want to know." Jules reached over and tucked a lock of my hair behind my ear. My body began to tremble.

The scent of him filled my nostrils, earthy and pungent. I could feel my heart beating, its rhythmic pulse sending blood to those other places yearning for his touch.

"Did you fuck him?" I had to ask the question.

"Does it excite you if I did?" He ran his thumb down the side of my face and across my lips, stopping atop them.

"Yes." I opened my mouth, taking his probing thumb on my tongue and suckling it.

His fingers tracked up the bridge of my nose and across my cheek, halting at the pulse point beside my ear. I could hear moaning as I continued to caress his thumb with my tongue; it came from me.

Jules removed his thumb, and without further warning replaced it with his hungry mouth and tongue. Tasting him, my body exploded in a shudder of delight. My hands ran up the sides of his soft shirt, hunting for the warm, taut flesh I knew resided beneath its crimson layer.

He released my mouth, leaving his nose touching my own. My breath came in short, shallow pants.

"I've wanted you for such a long, long time." He stroked my hair, pushing it away from my flushed face.

"I know."

"But you've stayed away from me?" He sounded hurt. I lay down on the bed and pulled him closer. He lay perched over me on his elbows.

"There are so many people who want a piece of you," I

said.

"You're scared there won't be enough of me to go around?"

"No." I shook my head. "I'm frightened that being with you will change everything - that it won't work out and then I'll be alone and have to leave."

Jules settled atop of me, stroking my cheek with the back of his hand. It felt cool on my warm skin.

He kissed me again, his bulk sinking slowly down on me, trapping me on the mattress. I lost myself in him as I'd done so very many times before while watching him from the side of the stage. Only this time there was just the two of us, no thousands of screaming fans wishing they were where I was now. I felt secure and loved at the center of his universe.

"I wouldn't let you go." Jules kissed me again, allowing his full weight to pin me to the bed. "Now I have you I'm never going to let you leave."

"It might all go terribly wrong and you'll be in a hurry to get rid of me." I stretched up with my lips to touch his again; he held them just out of reach above me, teasing me, making me work harder to touch him.

Relenting, he let our lips collide and the full weight of him came crashing down on me again. He forced his tongue deep into the recesses of my mouth. I took it in, clamoring for more of him. My hands snaked under his shirt, pushing the fabric up so I could play with the hardened expanse of his back.

My fingernails raked across the span of his shoulder muscles; he moaned and flinched, lifting himself briefly from me and giving me a moment to catch my breath.

He smiled at me, a rakish and charming smile - the

smile I'd seen him use to seduce 80,000 screaming fans. I suddenly remembered there would be hundreds of thousands of others I'd have to compete with for his attentions.

I pulled him back toward me.

"I won't ever want to get rid of you. I've waited far too long to do this to you," he reassured me, leaning sideways, allowing a hand to run up my side and stopping to cup my small breast.

My nipple reacted, springing forth like the first tiny bud of the pussy willow in spring.

"You like that."

I could feel myself blushing, heat radiating across my face and chest. "I do."

He ran his thumb around the nipple, and even through the sheer T-shirt the touch set off a train of electrical impulses. Those impulses fueling my increasing desire. Desire that culminated in the wet, seeping sensation gathering between my legs.

I needed him.

I needed him in me.

I needed him in me now.

As if reading my thoughts, he whispered in my ear, "I want you."

"I want you too." I felt brazen, prepared to abandon myself completely to him. "Undress me."

He smiled. A new and intimate smile I'd never seen before. It turned me on even more.

"I thought you'd never ask."

He reached down and pulled my T-shirt over my head, leaving my bra between him and my engorging nipples.

His shirt followed at a rapid rate. I'd seen Jules naked

on many occasions, but now, this close, the expanse of black, curly hair on his chest aroused me as much as his hands and lips playing the length of my body.

I reached up, running my fingers through the coarse hair, my fingernails combing and parting the dark strands.

Julian's body came to life under my touch, the warmth and texture of a body I'd admired, dried and dressed now made available to me.

Available to me exclusively.

His hours spent working out for shows had toned his chest, the downy hair that I couldn't keep my hands away from contrasting with the rigid muscle beneath.

He reached around behind me, struggling with the clasp on my bra. I didn't care. He leaned closer, allowing me to nuzzle my face into the inviting surrounds of his chest.

The clasp came free and I felt the caress of air across my nipples.

Jules moaned.

His mouth immediately latched on to one nipple, suckling hard. I arched toward his mouth. He let go my nipple, breaking the suction with an audible pop, then traced his tongue across the valley and peak of my chest and began to lavish the same treatment on its partner. The abandoned moist nipple reacted to the cool rush of air; the feeling almost as exquisite as the nipple in Jules' attentive mouth.

Fresh waves of desire washed over me. I wanted him naked, needed to feel the hot caress of flesh on flesh.

Jules let my other nipple go.

"You're so beautiful." He kissed me on the lips, then on my forehead, before burrowing into the tender, sweet spot behind my ear.

My entire body trembled in anticipation.

Jules ran his hands across my belly, hesitating when he got to the button of my jeans, looking to me for consent.

I nodded.

He deftly undid the button, sliding the jeans away from my body and revealing the tiny lace panties beneath.

He moaned again, the sound almost muffled as his mouth covered the white lace. A surge of energy and lust raced through me and I arched myself toward him, struggling to kick free the jeans that had a tight hold on my ankles, preventing me from opening my legs and allowing him full, unfettered reign over me.

Abandoning my aching loins, Jules pulled away from me, relieving me of the tangle of denim at my feet and then tearing at his own jeans. They came away easily, taking his boxers with them.

I couldn't take my eyes away from his engorged cock. It stood tall and firm, running parallel up his belly with the line of dark hair that joined his navel to his nether regions.

He leaned up over me again, his cock achingly close to my belly. Kissing me, he positioned himself between my legs, the coarse hairs on his brushing against my sensitive inner thighs. He lowered his solid cock against my waiting belly and I closed my mouth around his tongue and my legs around his thighs.

A flood of liquid escaped from me.

Jules released my mouth, panting and flushed in the face.

"I want you inside of me," I gasped. "Please, just take my pants off."

Flicking an expert thumb through the thin side strap, he

had my panties on the floor before I knew it.

Jules held himself over me.

"The drawer, by the side of the bed." He gestured toward the night stand.

Now wallabies moved at pace, in silence, across the Australian outback. I caught sight of them over Jules' lowered shoulder.

"What about the drawer?"

"Condom."

I struggled, but couldn't stretch as far as the drawer and was unable to dislodge myself from under his now sweating bulk. "I can't reach."

Jules hitched himself up along my body, enough so I was able to shuffle down and catch his cock in my mouth.

It was hard and smooth and I suckled it deep into the recesses of my mouth.

"Oh, dear God," Jules moaned.

I could feel him fighting to reach the drawer above me, but didn't give him a moment's respite from my sucking mouth.

He eased himself back down my body a little, so I assumed he must have reached a condom. I didn't let him go. I continued with rhythmic sliding of his cock into my mouth, more and more excited by his heightened reactions.

Jules' hips began to rock to the rhythm of my lips. I tilted my head slightly, looking up, meeting the intense green of his eyes. His face, flushed and with small beads of sweat breaking out around his temples, spoke silently of pleasure.

"You have to stop. I can't stand it." Jules tried to remove himself from the tortuous grip of my mouth and tongue, but my hand was too quick for him. I cupped his balls, digging my fingernails into the spongy skin at the base.

He moaned again, almost incoherently. "Mags. Please. Stop."

I held him tight, in mouth and in hand.

Ceased all movement.

The only sound was his heavy breathing. Still the wildlife trekked across the outback in silence.

"Oh, God. Let me go." His voice, a mere growl.

I released his wet cock from my mouth, but didn't release the claw-like grip I had on his balls. His cock stood before me, shimmering, the bulbous head almost purple.

"I've let you go. Now I want you inside of me."

He shuddered. The effect was as if a small fault line had run across the surface of his muscles.

Watching him, naked, beautiful and full of lust, my excitement mounted.

He ripped open the silver packet he held in his hand and extracted an opaque pink condom. He moved to put it on but I stopped him. "Let me. I want to do it."

I looked up as he handed me the small capsule. His entire body quivered.

He sat back, in the space between my legs. I shimmied out from under the imposing bulk of his charged body and took a firm hold of his cock in my hand.

More moaning.

I licked the dripping tip of his cock, drinking in the warm, masculine scent of him. His member pulsed in my palm at the touch of my tongue.

Exhilarated, I began the long, slow and sensuous unfurling of the condom down his shaft. The smell of rubber mingled with the aroma of him.

Jules watched me intently during this process. Squirming at my touch, little moans escaping his lips as the rubber tracked down the sensitive spine of his shaft.

I nestled the edge of the condom into the forest of black hair at the base camp of the mountain that was his cock. I ran my hands back over the flesh of his belly and up to the scrubland of his chest beyond.

He lay back on the bed, surrendering himself to me. I'd dreamed for so long to be here and now, to have him naked before me, willing to do my bidding. It excited me beyond belief.

I kissed him and positioned myself above his encased and powerful cock. Anticipation filling me to bursting point. I could barely wait to feel the full extent of him inside of me.

Jules held my hips, tantalizingly close to him, preventing me from moving forward and impaling myself on him.

"Are you sure?" The question and the tone of his voice touched me.

I nodded. "Yes."

He guided me then toward the peak of him. Releasing his grip on my hips and giving me full control.

I took a breath and plunged forward.

We gasped in unison. The feeling of him within me was exquisite.

I slid, back and forth over him, the sensations indescribable. I felt complete with him inside of me. The ache for him intensified and so did the speed with which I moved up and down on him.

I leaned further back so I could take him further into me.

Jules groaned, thrusting up with his hips, almost trying to dig himself into me.

I rode him like a bronco rider, his eager thrusting driving me to the tipping place and a near explosion of ecstasy.

Without missing a beat of our frenzied rhythm, Jules grabbed my forearms and pulled me down on top of him. His lips were on mine in an instant and his tongue found the deep recesses of my mouth, as his cock found the deep recess of my cunt.

I moaned around his intruding tongue. Overcome by the flood of an early orgasm.

Jules pushed me harder. "Keep coming for me." His voice was thick with lust, emotion etched on his beautiful face.

A fleeting thought that I might have some control if I remained on top of him vanished.

I surrendered to the dark side of my personality, to the overpowering feelings of pleasure, and ultimately surrendered control to Jules.

He flipped me like a rag doll. In a moment I was pinned under his bulk and he continued to hammer himself into me.

I loved it. The feeling of him above me, his toned and muscular body flaying me, driving me further and further into the oblivion of ecstasy.

He kissed me again. Roughly, consuming me with his mouth.

I met his every thrust. I met his every kiss and he met my every need and desire.

The rhythm between us built.

I felt another craving for him.

Our eyes locked.

His muscles began to spasm.

"Come for me." I needed him to relinquish himself to me. I wanted to feel I had total control of him.

Jules dropped his jaw into my collarbone.

I felt the hard, cold clamp of his teeth on my flesh.

The sharp pain of his bite.

My body went into spasm. A rolling orgasm took me.

The last vestige of Jules' control was smashed.

He released my shoulder and roared.

The tension between us abated. He fell on his side and snuggled me into him.

Our lust sated, we floated off to sleep.

CHAPTER TEN

I drifted out of a blissful doze to see Jules leaning up on one elbow, watching me.

I smiled.

"You're perfect." He stroked my hair away from my cheek, his fingers lingering around my earlobe.

We lay naked and content. I loved him. I knew that much. All thoughts of Nick had gone from my mind. I knew I was exactly where I was supposed to be in the universe at this moment.

The Discovery channel continued to play its kaleidoscope of silent animal movies on the other side of the room. I thought about the amount of time I spent with Jules in front of a plethora of menagerie. Hours and hours of whale, beaver, bird and bear. He had an amazing soft spot for all kinds of critters and seemed to connect with them on some spiritual level I failed to understand.

Perhaps that was why he could connect with a forty-thousand-strong audience, yet struggled with intimate one-on-one relationships. It occurred to me we'd just made a massive leap on the one-to-one front.

It always fascinated me, the relationship he had with his audience en masse. How he enchanted them with his music. He touched so many. The emails and letters, proposals of marriage, thanks for saving lives were all testament to his gift.

The songs he and Frederick composed, their lyrics and rhythms changed people. How did that all work?

Lying beside me now, he didn't seem like some modern-day messiah.

A lot of musicians in the business behaved as if they were Jesus reincarnated, but Jules wasn't one of them. He had terrible fears and anxiety. His self-doubt was legendary.

Jules now found himself in the difficult position of being someone who had, in the early days, desperately wanted fame, needing to feel the adoration of a crowd - almost feeding on it.

But now he wanted it all to go away. He missed being able to walk down the street without being stared at. He missed just being able to pop down the road to buy a packet of chewing gum.

He could no longer go anywhere without being accosted by someone who wanted a tiny piece of him.

It was an exhausting way to live.

No wonder he escaped with the Discovery animals; at least with them he had some peace and quiet. Something sorely lacking in his exposed and open existence.

He often told me God's gift to him was his voice and his writing talent – and that his gift back to God was using that talent. What he hadn't bargained for was the unforeseen price musicians pay for being adored by their

115

public.

"Where are you, my lovely?" Jules fingers meandered down the valley between my breasts and then circled my navel.

I shuddered, the little hairs along the line of my tummy lifting toward his magnetic touch.

"I'm thinking how hard life is for you."

He ran his tongue from my navel down that small sensitive strip, pausing above the cropped line of my pubic hair.

"Life isn't hard." I could feel the warmth of his breath above my slowly swelling labia. "Not while I'm here with you, like this."

His tongue lingered along the length of my pubic hair, just touching my outer labia with its wet tip.

I flinched - not in pain, but in pure delight.

"I didn't mean exactly at this minute." I struggled to keep a hold of coherent thought as he continued to tickle my most private parts with his tongue.

"What did you mean?" He paused to look at me, teasing me.

"Please don't stop."

"I don't intend to, but I want you to talk to me, tell me what you were thinking."

"It's hard to think rationally when you're doing that to me."

"Try."

He poked his tongue back into my sensitive reaches. Pushing further in.

Heat rushed to my cheeks and chest. My nipples rose in small, knotted peaks.

"I was thinking about how you can't just walk down the

street without being hounded."

His mouth began to work my swelling labia.

Blood poured from my extremities to my engorged lips.

My fingers began to tingle.

My breathing became shallow.

Jules stopped to speak. "I can't walk down the street."

I didn't want him to talk, didn't want him to cease his ministrations.

"Don't stop." He didn't begin again. "Please, Jules."

"Tell me more about what you were thinking."

"I was thinking how every time somebody wants something from you-" he began to lick me again "-they take a little from you." His probing tongue dipped back into me. I squirmed, lifting my hips toward the heat of his mouth. "And how it's not a lot people want. A smile, a handshake, a picture."

I moaned. His finger had found the inside of my cunt. Expertly he nudged the sensitive wall side spot inside of me.

I couldn't help grinding into him.

Jules lifted his mouth away. Cool air touched wet skin. He said, "It's like little, soft balls being thrown at you; one on its own doesn't hurt, neither do hundreds, but you get very tired of being hit all the time."

"I can understand that." I was desperate for him to re-engage his mouth between my legs, and from the look on his face he knew it. "Please, don't make me beg."

He spread my lips, sucking on my clit as his lubricated finger found its way into my tight ass.

The wave of ecstasy came from nowhere, closely followed by orgasm.

He worked my body like he worked a crowd. With no

mercy.

Orgasm after orgasm rolled over the plateau of my body. He didn't desist for a second and my body, wracked by intense pleasure, became slack and pliable under him.

His mouth and fingers released me. I floated in a sea of delicious feelings, drunk on the passion flowing through me.

In what seemed like no more than a moment, he flipped my legs up over his shoulders, almost doubling me in two. My thighs touched my breasts and all I knew was the overwhelming sensation of Jules' hard cock plunging deep into me, the tip banging into my cervix, filling me to capacity.

I moaned again. My breath came in short, sharp bursts, my lungs full to exploding. All I could comprehend was the bulk of him overpowering me. In me. On me. Taking me.

"Fuck me," I panted. "Fuck me hard."

He needed no further encouragement.

Thrusting firm and fast into me, every stroke moved me a little further back up the bed.

He kept his ground. Ploughing into me.

Harder.

Faster.

Deeper.

My head came to rest against the thick material headboard.

His green eyes were wild with lust.

"Don't stop," I moaned.

He pushed into me.

Rough.

Savage.

"I. Want. To. Make. You. Come." Each word came out individually, atop a wave of Jules's thrusting cock.

The veins on the side of his throat and temples stood out, a harsh blue against the flushed pink of his face. Beads of sweat formed on his top lip, others ran in little rivers down the sides of his temples.

A small pool of water accumulated in the cavity between my breasts.

Still he pushed into me.

Still my hips rose to meet him.

"Oh, God." The words, guttural, came from a carnal place within him.

"Come for me, gorgeous." I coaxed his climax from him as I coaxed him onto stage each evening.

"Oh, Lord."

"Come on, don't fight it."

"It's so sweet."

I dug my fingernails into the soft flesh of his ass.

He moaned, almost incoherent.

I watched his struggle, his desperate need to hold off the tidal wave of pleasure threatening his control.

"Come for me, my lover." I almost whispered the words, but he heard me.

Our eyes connected. He lost it, surrendering to me and coming on my command.

Lost in me and the sea of his desire, he shuddered.

The control, the vision of him, and my own self-will dissolved. His climax subsided, replaced by mine. My vision blurred, a sharp spike of light exploded above Jules' head, and I felt a connection with something much greater than the two of us. An overwhelming energy and beauty I couldn't describe took a hold of me, transporting me beyond the bounds of our simple bodies.

Did I pass out? An urgent hammering on the bedroom door dragged me back to consciousness.

"Oh, God - who's that, I wonder?" Jules lay on his back, the crisp white linen sheet draped artistically across his loins. I had the urge to rip it off and start all over again with him.

"Ignore them. They'll go away." I snuggled spoon-like against his body, his arm tucked under my neck, his hand stretching down to my lower back, while my fingers caressed the thick, dark mat of his chest hair.

I sighed contentedly, refusing to move a muscle.

The banging continued, getting more urgent.

"Fuck off!" Jules' yell jolted my neck, disturbing my tranquility.

"I need to talk to Mags."

"What does he want?" I could recognize the foghorn tone of Dan's voice even through the mahogany door.

"She's busy. Fuck off, Dan."

"Maybe I should go and sort him out." I certainly didn't want to leave the security and tranquility of my spot next to Jules, but this fantasy did have to come to an end at some point.

"No." Jules was firm.

"You're not having reality crash in on us then?"

"That's right."

"It's going to eventually, you know." I wriggled closer to his warm body. I felt the sheets move as his cock responded to me.

He rolled onto his hip. "Well, it's not going to barge in right at the present moment."

"Oh, and why's that then?"

He pushed his hard cock against my stomach. "Because I simply haven't had my fill of you yet."

"He needs to save the whales." Dan looked at me in all seriousness.

"You're kidding, right?" Trying to have a conversation with Dan while pretending I hadn't just spent the last six hours locked in Jules' bedroom was difficult.

"No, I'm not."

Dan, to give him his due, tried to carry on as if it was business as usual, but he looked at me with a knowing glint in those gray eyes. Everyone else seemed happy to continue with the charade too, although in the deep recesses of my mind - and those deeper places where I could still feel Jules inside of me - I could tell they all knew.

"Whales. Is this some kind of seventies, throw-back, hippie idealism?"

"No, it's not. Whales are very hip at the moment."

"How do you work that one out?"

I was working really hard not to think about those chafed parts of my body that longed to be chafed some more.

"There's just recently been a summit in the Pacific, so it's very relevant in the area."

"I know we're going to the Pacific, it's an easy fit, but aren't there plans for Jules to tour Japan early next year? An attack on their whaling policy isn't going to go down too well at all." I thought whales were a ridiculous idea. "Why can't we just go on some mission about global warming or our carbon footprint like everyone else does?"

"Because-" Dan's voice took on his serious tone "-as well you know, your dearest Julian is a Discovery channel addict and if we can work an angle with the network he'll be back on top again."

Dan winked when he said 'back on top'. I could feel myself blush.

I pulled him aside into the kitchen area of the suite, away from the prying ears of the others. Jules, bless him, had refused to come out of his bedroom. As usual, I'd been sent out to face everyone. He'd peddled me some moronic excuse about emerging later, when the fuss over me had died down and they'd leave him alone.

"Besides, the Japanese will have forgotten all about it by the time we get there and, quite frankly, Jules' demographic are young and pretty much against eating whale meat anyway."

"The thought of eating whale makes me want to puke."

Dan lifted my hand and looked at my scrawny forearm. "The thought of eating anything tends to make you puke."

No secrets on tour. Why did I believe Jules and I could get together without the entire universe knowing about it?

At that moment Jules strolled into the room, put his arm nonchalantly around my waist and kissed me on the cheek.

I don't know who blushed more furiously, Dan or me.

"What's up that you had to get us out of bed, Dan?" Jules threw down the gauntlet.

I could have kicked him for being so shameless - but I shouldn't have expected anything else from a man who we were trying to save from the ravages of the tabloids due to his questionable sexual conquests.

It hit me. Why didn't that bother me?

Maybe he wasn't the only shameless person in the room.

Dan, whom I expected to have the temerity to brazen it out, collapsed into a bumbling and blushing heap.

"We're off to save the whales, it appears." Why I should have felt the need to step in and cover Dan's dithering arse escaped me. My mind was too full of Jules...those questionable sexual conquests... Did they include me? And what the hell was I going to do about the straitlaced ex-husband of mine jetting his way back to Dubai?

"Great." Jules seemed genuinely pleased. "Which ones?"

"What do you mean, which ones?" Dan slowly came back to his senses.

"Minke whales, pilot whales, sperm whales." Jules gave me a small hug; he hadn't let go of my side. "I need to know which species we're campaigning for."

"Who the fuck knows? They're whales, for Christ's sake."

"It's important, Dan. We need to make sure this is credible - don't we, Mags?"

I nodded. "We do."

The enormity of the afternoon's lovemaking with Jules began hammering at my psyche. Familiar feelings of revulsion reared in the battleground of my mind.

"Excuse me, guys." I needed to escape from the claustrophobic feelings crowding in on me.

"You okay?" Jules, bless him, looked concerned.

"You've gone awfully pale." Dan mirrored his anxiety.

"Maybe you need something to eat. I'm starving." Jules had an ironclad stomach, except for those few moments before he got on stage every night.

"Mags starving - are you kidding?" Dan looked at Jules with disbelief in his eyes.

"Well, I am. Come on, we need something to eat. Let's go out." Jules moved me skillfully away from Dan and the kitchen.

"You hate going out," I said. "I think I might just go and have a lie down." A sense of nausea overcame me. The consequence of our afternoon together, or the realization that I hadn't managed to hide my unhealthy attitude toward eating from Jules, I couldn't be sure.

"Forget food, I'm coming for another lie down?" Jules said.

Despite the growing feelings of guilt threatening to overcome me, his delight at our newfound status as lovers filled my soul.

"I need a shower as well. I don't think we smell too good."

"I'm happy to help with that too." He nuzzled the side of my neck. "You smell fine to me."

"No. You go and get yourself something to eat and I'll sort myself out."

"You okay, Mags?" His concern touched me.

"I'll be fine. It's a lot to deal with, Jules."

"I know. I know it is." He caressed my cheek with his hand. Those warm feelings flooded back over me. I felt safe and secure when he touched me.

"After I've eaten, why don't I bring something in to you later?"

"That would be nice. Thanks."

I retired to my room, a maelstrom of thoughts whirling through my mind.

By myself, in the privacy of my own bathroom, I began

to shake, aware that not more than six or seven hours earlier my husband had stood in the very same room with a bloody nose. Overwhelmed by anxiety, I dropped to my knees in front of the toilet. What little I had consumed food-wise in the earlier part of the day evacuated itself.

Spent from both the lovemaking and the post-coital anxiety, I stripped and allowed the hot water of the rain-shower to wash over me. I knew the water could wash away the residue of Jules from my skin, but it wouldn't erase him from my mind; nor was it going to resolve the issue of Nick.

I'd never been unfaithful before. In all the years I'd been touring and all the years Nick had been traveling I'd never been with another man. I tried to tell myself the marriage was over. He'd said so himself, before he walked out.

I didn't know if Nick had been with another woman and I knew thinking about that now was just my way of trying to assuage my guilt. I struggled with an overwhelming sense of shame. For breaking a sacred promise and for the hurt it would cause.

I thought about how happy I'd been when we first married, full of optimistic hope for a bright future together. We took vows, promising to love each other until death us do part.

I thought about our home, the trinkets I'd collected on my travels and filled it with. The tapestry of our life, interwoven over many years. The shower washed away the tears I cried for the life I'd wanted and hadn't been able to build with the man I'd married.

I thought about the consequences of my afternoon of divine lovemaking with Jules. How it consummated the destruction and dissolution of my marriage and my future life with Nick.

I may have enjoyed an afternoon of ecstasy, but now I would hurt and mourn for the life I'd just left behind.

I thought about my life touring with Jules. How much I loved the tight group we'd become. How special my relationships were with each and every member of the crew - the band, the dancers, the stage crew, the roadies, Dan, Frederick, everyone.

Nothing could ever be the same. I'd taken a series of actions that would change my life, Jules' life and Nick's life forever. The fallout from an afternoon in bed was gargantuan.

All I could do was deal with the consequences the best I could. It reminded me of a physics lesson I'd had at school years ago. For every action there was a positive and equal reaction. No matter which way I moved now, there had been a shift that couldn't be ignored or overlooked; it could only be overcome.

I turned the shower off, pulled the warm towel from the heated towel rail and wrapped it around my body. Drying myself off, I grabbed the white fluffy robe from the hook behind the door, encased myself in the warm and comforting fabric and put myself to bed.

Still, when I closed my eyes I felt him all over me. My skin tingled, my body longed for his touch. I knew he'd come again to me tonight after the show and I could barely contain my anticipation for when he would lie naked with me again. In the meantime, I had to steal myself for getting him up on that stage.

CHAPTER ELEVEN

I took up my usual position backstage in the tight circle; the mantra had begun. All thoughts of what had happened earlier in the day were suspended. We were one; this was about the crowd out there and the experience we would give them.

No matter what happened in our personal lives, we were professionals. Nothing got in the way of ensuring that the punters who'd paid big bucks to be here got the experience they'd paid for.

We all put our personal demons, fears and lives aside and worked for the good of the tour.

"... and the wisdom to know the difference. Thank, you. Thank you."

The harmonious chant done, we all separated, heading for our pre-show perches. I moved with Jules, his ever-present shadow in the wings. The atmosphere was no different than it had been for the last 147 shows we'd done. There wasn't a flicker or hint from either of us that our love had been consummated that afternoon. The ever-increasing threat of depression rolled over me in unrelenting waves.

I had Jules' small bucket in my hands. He leaned over, emptying the contents of his stomach as he did before every show.

In a state of almost tantric grace, I wiped his mouth as I had done the previous 147 times, placed the bucket in the wings and held his hand, waiting for his cue.

He jiggled uncontrollably at my side. It reminded me of the way his body had behaved when he came this afternoon. I scolded myself for having that thought at this moment, then wondered if he might be thinking the same thing.

Cue music, crowd roar. Jules let go of my hand to head for the stage.

Then he stopped.

Turned.

Looked at me.

The world froze for a millisecond.

"I love you." The words I'd longed to hear him say.

"You're on," I said.

He stood, rooted to the spot. Waiting for me to say something else.

"I love you too. Now, go!"

His face lit up, matching the ferocity of the lights bathing the stage.

He scurried on. Late. But the crowd didn't care.

They worshipped him.

I worshipped him.

We were all in trouble.

"I don't think I can do this, Jules." The words that earlier today I'd felt sure would never come forth from my mouth.

He'd arrived in my room, post-show, with a platter of fruit and dipping chocolate in an attempt to tempt me into eating something.

The show had gone well. The all-important crowd loved every single minute of him and more essential to our livelihood, he'd loved every minute of being in front of them.

I'd watched from my usual spot on this tour, in the wings. As he worked the crowd, my love and respect for him crystallized. While the crowd roared and screamed for him, he'd look and find me, wink, or blow a small kiss. He included me and made me a part of the wonderful creation that was Julian on stage. I felt a sense of belonging and love I'd never felt in my life. Yet, faced with the cold, hard reality of untangling my prior life, a nagging despair descended over me like a gray, clinging mist.

Jules sensed this and did his best to dispel the clouds of my doubt.

"We haven't done anything wrong. We love each other." He looked desperate, clearly determined he wasn't going to let me slip from his grasp.

"I'm married, in case you've forgotten that fact."

"Married, shmarried. Besides, he's left you." He waved his hand dismissively. "You guys have only been married in name for years. Don't try and kid me that it's been anything other than companionship."

He popped a chocolate-dipped strawberry in his mouth, the red juice and a sliver of chocolate sliding down his chin.

"And a pretty spasmodic companionship at that." I

needed someone else's perspective on my marriage. I just wondered if Jules was the right person.

I reached over and collected the sliver of strawberry and chocolate from the side of his mouth. He suckled the juice and chocolate from my finger. Triggering in me a sense of desire and longing for him.

He wasn't the right person to be talking to about my life at all.

I allowed him to feed me pieces of chocolate-dipped fruit, but all the while the nagging feelings of depression and darkness were clawing to get in around the light and brightness he brought to my life.

I continued to push them to the back of my mind, those tendrils of bleakness that threatened to take up permanent residence, like mold spores settling on a slice of bread.

"I really shouldn't be talking to you about Nick."

"Why not?" He seemed unperturbed by what I believed to be the ridiculous situation we found ourselves.

"Because you're not exactly an independent observer, are you?"

"I don't know." He fed me a slice of mango he'd half dipped in the chocolate. I wasn't a fan of food in any form, but he was managing to coax a large portion of the platter into me this way. "I think I'm the best person to talk to about this because I love you and want you so much."

"Exactly." I could feel the food taking up residence in my usually empty stomach. The feeling was warm and comforting, much like having my new Jules around.

It dawned on me how comfortable and at ease I was around Jules. A long time ago we'd slipped into the life of a working married couple, but without the added extra spice of sex. I'd made the decision to allow Jules to seduce me and immediately felt better.

I picked up a strip of pineapple, dipped the tip of it in chocolate and popped it into my mouth.

"I'm pleased to see you eating something."

I looked up, startled. I hated people watching me eat.

"Don't stop now. I know you don't like eating around anyone."

"Well..."

Jules held his hands up. "There's no need to explain yourself. Like I'm not neurotic enough for the both of us." He stroked my cheek with his hand and I couldn't help nuzzling into the touch. "But I do worry about your food intake. I've been around enough dancers and backup singers to know what an eating disorder looks like."

Anger immediately flared inside of me. "I don't have a disorder."

"Right." He nodded his head knowingly. "Like it's normal to avoid eating in front of people and then only eat enough to keep a sparrow alive.

"Sparrows eat three times their own bodyweight a day."

He laughed. "That's a myth and you and I know it, and it's spun out by every anorexic teenager in the world."

"You calling me an anorexic teenager?"

"No. I'm just saying that, like me, you have to work at eating."

"Like you?"

"Why do you think I'm such an expert at throwing up before a show?"

"I just thought it was nervousness." It felt strange, learning new things about Jules. I'd thought I knew everything about him.

"I trained myself to vomit on command years ago."

I thought about the amount of rubbish he consumed before the start of a show. It had never occurred to me that some time in his past he might have been bulimic.

"I didn't think men suffered from bulimia."

"There are lots of things that men suffer from that you don't know about, and lots of things about me you don't know either."

"So how come you still behave like that before a show?"

He tilted his head sideways, looking up at me from under bushy eyebrows.

"So how come I still have to come in here armed with fruit and chocolate in case there's any chance whatsoever of persuading you to put some food into that poor undernourished body of yours?"

"Touché."

I took a small wedge of mandarin from the platter. "So we're both neurotic, don't drink and misbehave around food."

"And around each other." He ran a sticky piece of mango across my lips before popping it into his own mouth.

"Well, I can tell you now-" I eyed the remains of the fruit platter warily "-I'm officially refusing to engage in sex with you, chocolate and the fruit platter."

He looked at me mock crestfallen. "Oh, you are such a spoilt brat, and a spoilsport to boot."

"Come here." He put the platter away and settled himself on top of my bed. "Where would madam like to sleep tonight? In here or in my room?"

"Room is really an understatement - it's the royal suite."

And particularly grand when compared to my box

room.

"We could just stay here." I checked the small clock on the nightstand. Nearly 2am in God-only-knew what time zone. I'd lost track months ago. A doziness overcame me; the food or the long day, I wasn't sure which, but I needed to sleep. Jules still seemed high and tense from the show, but I knew I could wind him down with a little effort.

"Are they all out there?" I'd declined the quiet game of post-show cards in favor of retreating to my room to be by myself with my professed misery. But I still felt uncomfortable about the team knowing what was going on between Jules and me.

"Just Otis. Everyone else has gone to bed, or taken off for a night on the tiles."

"Ugh." I couldn't think of anything worse than a night out. Many of the band traded on the fact that Jules' fans would be in the local bars, hoping he'd come out to play. As Frederick so aptly put it, they were able to pick up women they'd never normally have a chance with, just by being members of Jules' band.

Apart from his wild night with Young Elvis and Barbie, Jules spent most of his post-show evenings playing cards and drinking tea. Hardly the public's perceived life of a rock God.

I think that was what annoyed me so much about the way the press crucified him. I'd driven him to act completely out of character, yet they jumped on the chance to make a lousy dollar selling their fish-and-chip wrappers.

"So, what you're saying is if we spend the night in your room I wouldn't have to run the gauntlet."

"No need to traipse past the rest of the traveling circus."

I laughed. I hadn't laughed for a long time.

"So you admit you're at the head of a traveling circus, then?"

"Absa-bloody-lutely." He grinned.

Considering I felt on the brink of descending into the depths of darkness, his light and obvious delight in being with me acted as a lifeline, keeping me anchored to him at the top of the cliff. "I guess we'd best make a run for it then, before it's time for them to start straggling in for brunch."

"That's my girl." He pulled me to my feet and then slapped me decisively on the rump.

"Less of the slap and tickle."

"I haven't even started with you yet."

My chocolate-and-fruit-filled stomach did a little turn. He took my hand and led me out of my room and into my new life with him.

As we reached his door and I passed through into his domain, I could only hope the rest of the world was ready for the change.

Gazing out of the elevated window of the first-class deck, I saw atolls sitting like jewels in the acres of blue water below me, spots of green ringed by bands of what I imagined was sand. The islands were scattered, as if someone had thrown a small handful of green marbles across an aqua sandpit.

Plumes of smoke rose above the biggest landmass generated by huge fires below. From my investigative reading, I knew this must be fields of burning sugar cane.

The large island looked rugged and dark in the fading light. High mountains sat in the middle and coconut palms grew randomly throughout the wild, lush landscape.

"Look at it! It looks just like it does on the National Geographic channel." An excited Julian held my hand as our plane made its approach into Nadi airport. It seemed right and comfortable to be with him and to be holding his hand. We'd agreed to put the chaos of the last few days behind us and concentrate on having some rest, away from the prying eyes of the media. We'd also taken a step back from the tension of the suite encounter and decided on being simply friends again and it felt safe and good.

Bereft-looking, tumbledown shacks lined the airport runway, some with traditional thatched roofs, others with layers of iron assembled in the same manner.

"It looks a bit third world. Are you sure this is going to be okay?" Frederick poked his head around the seat from behind us.

The tight, close-knit crew were here - it was a term of the contract that we take some time together to relax and regroup. Sheree sat on the other side of the plush aircraft with Otis. He'd taken a shine to her since the night everyone had gone out on the town and seemed to be protecting her. It made me wonder what else might have happened that night that I wasn't privy to.

"Oh, my God," I exclaimed. "The fires are burning right up to the side of the runway. How can that be okay with jets coming in here?"

"I'm sure you don't have to worry." Jules squeezed my hand. "Truckloads of tourists come in and out of here and I don't remember Fiji ever appearing on an episode of *Air Crash Investigation*." He was a mine of useless information, most of it derived from hours of watching documentaries.

We settled ourselves in for the landing. The lone

stewardess who attended to our needs in first class had gotten over her dumbstruck schoolgirl stage and largely left us alone, but only after Jules posed for photographs. I hated how the public felt as if they had ownership rights to him. Everyone wanted a slice, as if he were being chipped away molecule by molecule.

If I wanted to be a permanent part of his life I knew it was something I'd have to come to terms with. I just didn't know how.

We disembarked from the plane and heat hit me as if God had opened the door of some universal oven. My body responded by breaking out into a sweat. I could feel the pores on my face opening and liquid gathering on the end of my nose.

"You didn't tell us we were coming to an outdoor sauna." Frederick's thin frame wilted under the oppressive heat. Even though the sun was beginning to set at the end of the runway the temperature remained intolerably high.

"Pack any board shorts?" I'd been trying to tell him his usual uniform of black jeans and T-shirt wasn't going to cut it in the tropics. Clearly he hadn't taken my advice.

"The lengths you'll go to get him out of black denim amazes me." Dan swatted a miniscule flying insect away from his face.

Mynah birds gathered in the dusk light on the sills of the airport terminal. Otis eyed the flocks suspiciously. I remembered his phobia of all things feathered and wondered how he'd coped as a soldier in the jungle. The birds, in their hundreds, lined the outside of the concrete bridge we walked over. It led us to a small gangway, and through and beyond to the terminal proper. By international standards it was third world, and having come from the plush surrounds of first class it seemed as if we'd walked into a concrete bus terminal.

Inside the hot, tin shelter we were met by a trio of guitar-strumming and singing Fijians in blue-and-white hibiscus shirts.

"Get a load of them." Frederick stopped in his tracks. His appreciation of anything musical, however ethnic, coming to the fore.

"Mess up too many times on this tour, pal, and you could be over there singing harmony with them." Jules poked Frederick in the ribs.

"I don't know." Frederick held his fingertips to his temples and closed his eyes, as if looking into the future. "I can see you singing lead for them and living in one of those shacks down the side of the runway." The two of them never missed a chance to tease.

"I think it sounds lovely and you two clowns should take some notice. Maybe you can work certain parts of the underlying melodies into some of your new tracks."

They both looked at me, bewilderment painted on their faces, almost as if I'd just suggested we purchase one of the nasty plastic coconut palms adorning the holding pen they called customs.

The entire area was a shambolic mess, with lines of people zigzagging backwards and forwards between strips of blue tape. The local Fijians in one row – others strewn across the airport lounge lizard-like.

"Where the hell is the processing for first-class passengers?" Julian scanned the crowded room for any sign of an elite holding area.

"It appears to be every man, woman and child for

themselves," I noted.

Otis and Verne hung close to the two of us, on constant watch for anything or anyone who could have been a threat.

"What's the use of being let off the frigging plane first if there's a backlog from the last flight in front of us?" Dan looked at me. I'd known him long enough to register the flicker of tension growing in his voice.

"Don't worry about it. There's no one here who knows who the hell we are." I tried to sound reassuring.

"At the minute." He looked at his watch. "What's the local time here?"

I had reset my watch on the plane after the Captain's announcement. "It's ten past seven."

"You have got cars waiting for us, haven't you?"

"Of course I have. How long have I been organizing transfers for this traveling circus?"

"Just checking. I don't want to get stuck outside with this mob if anyone recognizes him."

Julian slouched by my side, assuming the role of a dejected twelve-year-old forced to go on the worst possible school outing. I could see the sweat trickling down the side of his face to the base of his jawline. Occasionally he would swipe at it like an irritated animal.

Slowly we shuffled our way to the front of the line.

"Bula!" The effusive Island greeting from the airport customs official brought us to attention. He was a burly Fijian, seemingly 17-foot tall and wearing a khaki shirt.

He took his time with my passport. Checking it carefully, fingering through the large number of pages. Because of the amount of travel we did, we always ordered passports with extra pages. He turned the document over a couple of times, testing its weight in his large hands. Satisfied, he then turned his attention to Jules' companion tome.

"Have you visited Fiji before, Mr MacAvoy?" The deep tenor of his voice seemed to vibrate through me as it navigated its way across the room.

"No." Jules had removed his hat and glasses for the customs check. I could tell he felt vulnerable and exposed.

"Ah, then you are in for a treat." Our customs man smiled. Huge white gravestone teeth gleamed at us from their deep brown surrounds.

After the wait for customs, I could tell that Jules wasn't so sure about that.

The customs official handed us a small blue piece of paper as he returned our documents. "Keep this with your passport; you will need it to leave the country."

My immediate thought was I'd have to collect everyone's passports and store them all in my room safe. Knowing this mob, they'd lose their blue pieces of paper and be stuck on this coral atoll for all eternity.

"By God, it's hot." Jules drooped by my side under the weight of his winter gear. I'd tried to prepare him and the rest of the complaining crew for the heat we'd encounter but they hadn't listened. We'd just come from a much cooler climate and everyone was cranky and hot.

We traversed baggage collection, which appeared to be even more chaotic. My thoughts were with the passengers traveling in cattle class. Our luggage rode the carousel first, sporting its bright-orange priority stickers.

"Ted. Over here." Frederick led the charge for luggage trolleys with Dan, wilting under the humid heat, a close second.   Otis didn't move more than a foot from me or Jules and sent Verne to organize transportation for our bags.

"Mags, remind me again why we thought it was a good idea to come here?" Jules was used to making it through an international airport in less than fifteen minutes.

"Because no one knows you here."

"True." His face brightened. Not a single person had accosted him since we'd disembarked.

"And once we get out of this godforsaken hole we'll be in a tropical paradise."

"I like the sound of that." He said.

Verne returned with a trolley stacked with my and Jules' luggage.   He and Otis traveled light and one of their knapsacks sat precariously balanced on our luggage pile. The other Verne wore on his back.

Otis grabbed his pack from the trolley and we were on the move again.

It felt like herding cats on speed, trying to corral the troops.   Far too much alcohol had been consumed on the flight, and with the prospect of a relaxing week ahead most of the crew carried a number of yellow duty-free bags which rattled at every lurching step.

I anticipated we would be another hour at least, trying to negotiate our way through baggage searches - and possibly, considering the state some of the crew were in, body searches to boot.

But I'd forgotten what third-world administrators were like; they never ceased to amaze me. To my delight, our bags were simply lifted over what could only be described a miniature fence in the middle of a table – it reminded me of an absurd game of luggage ping pong – and we were free to go.

As we left the terminal building I followed the map supplied by the agent and we soon found ourselves in another little concrete oven. The buildings were built to hurricane standard and with their white-and-blue lattice-work on the front reminded me of multistory parking buildings.

"Bula!" The agent for the resort greeted us as enthusiastically as the customs Official had.

"Must be the patent greeting here, you think? And check out the flowers. Very nice." Jules' irritation and exhaustion was beginning to make itself known.

"Sarcasm is the lowest form of wit - you know, that don't you?"

"Is there any chance you can get me to a nice air-conditioned van before I expire?" He stared at me, a sullen expression on his face.

"I'm working on it. You're not the only one who's hot and tired."

I directed my attention to the resort representative, anxious to get us away from here. I was aware of short, dark Indian men gathering in little groups by the stairs. They reminded me of the mynah birds assembled on the outside of the terminal building, all fighting for their night roost.

I shuddered.

Neither had they escaped Otis or Verne's attention, both keeping a close watch on the members of the numerous clusters.

"Welcome to Fiji." The agent, dressed in a brown wrap skirt complete with green hibiscus-flower print shirt, began the arduous process of presenting each of us with a tiny shell lei.

Each little cone shell, less than half the size of my fingernail, was strung to its neighboring shell, end to end. Fascinated, I wondered who'd spend hours stringing these shells together for the tourists.

The sun had set while we were incarcerated in the chaos they called customs. Eventually, I manage to shuffle myself, Julian and Otis into one of the small fleet of transport vehicles reserved for us.

"Ah, a nice piece of German engineering." Jules patted the cold leather interior of the Mercedes.

The sweet sickly scent of vehicles groomed for far too much public use in a tropical climate greeted me. Albeit a nice change from the equally sweet and sickly burning scent that infused the air around the airport - the aroma of burning sugar cane permeated everything.

"I don't know what's worse-" Otis screwed up his nose "-the smell in here or the smell out there."

"Well, at least it's not a hundred degrees in here." Jules had managed to plaster as much of himself against the cool leather seats as was humanly possible.

"What must their carbon footprint look like, with all that burning going on?"

Otis had never struck me as a conservationist. "Do you think the government cares?" I asked.

"There's not much of a government left," Otis pointed out. "They were all marched out of parliament at gunpoint not so long ago, remember?"

"Fuck! Is it safe for us to be here?" The gravity of the situation spurred Jules into extracting himself from the comfort of the icy seat and sit up and take notice.

"You don't think Otis or I would let you go anywhere

unsafe, do you?"

"I suppose not. But what - are the army running the place? Do we have to be locked in our rooms at dusk?"

Otis laughed. "No, mate, it's nothing like that. We just have to make sure we stay in the tourist areas. You'll be okay."

It occurred to me, as we drove through unlit streets where the only sign of life was the odd local walking alongside the dusty tracks they call roads, that we could disappear in the wilderness and no one would know.

True, we had Otis on hand with his survival training, but how would your average tourist call for help in a foreign land like this one? What screening process did the local drivers go through? How did we know our driver wasn't a serial killer and the three of us merely his next victims?

"Otis, are you sure you know we're going the right way?" I asked. "Everything looks the same to me."

"Yeah. Just pitch black." A helpful observation from Jules.

"Absolutely, you have nothing to worry about. I vetted the transportation and I can confirm we're on track to be there in about fifteen minutes."

Yes, we had the valuable screening process of Otis. I still wondered how the rest of the tourists fared.

CHAPTER TWELVE

We crossed a bridge and came to a barrier arm and checkpoint. It reminded me of crossing the border between European states. Someone who appeared to be of military occupation checked our driver's identification. A few words were passed in the local language, then with a friendly smile and wave the border-patrol guard lifted the barrier arm and waved us through.

"Security for the resort," Otis confirmed. "The entire area is a compact offshore island connected by the bridge at this one point. It means the locals are unable to infiltrate the space."

"What about by boat?" Jules had seen far too many modern-day pirate documentaries.

"We are far enough away from the mainland township that it's just too hard for them to get here by boat."

It sounded safe enough.

We snaked our way around the dimly lit roads. The whole island was obviously geared toward the tourist industry. From what little I'd seen of the squalid townships we passed through, this part of the country seemed well developed and struck me as being a sanitized-for-tourists development.

Pulling up at the neat, exclusive resort, I was struck by the interesting array of two-story apartment-block structures, complete with thatched roofs. A number of scattered thatched outbuildings completed the scene.

Our fleet of vehicles pulled up and the staff were waiting to greet us, standing in a semi-circle along the edge of a deeply polished dark-wood floor. I knew we'd all but booked out the entire resort, so we would be safe from the prying eyes of the public.

Jules and I stepped from the cool air-conditioned comfort of our vehicle. We were met not only by the warm and humid heat of the night, but also by the hearty sing-song greeting "Bula" from the gathered crowd. Then the drumming started. A huge Fijian man, with the tiniest frangipani flower tethered behind his ear, its bright white, yellow-edged petals contrasting against his short black hair, was beating the hell out of a hollow wooden drum.

"It's a bit naff, isn't it?" I hated all things touristy.

"Nah, it's ace," said Jules. He and Ted were transfixed, both applauding loudly when the drumming ended.

Bloody musos!

"Welcome. Please let us get you a cold drink while we arrange for your luggage to go to your rooms." The articulate Indian clerk shook our hands and took us through to a charming room overlooking a central courtyard.

We sat perched above a man-made waterfall, which fell into a huge pool below. The sound of rushing water precluded much in the way of conversation.

I decided sitting quietly probably wasn't such a bad

thing. Jules still seemed wrecked from the tour and from the fallout around the Young Elvis and Barbie incident. The press just hadn't been able to leave it alone. I refused to talk about it anymore. The added stress of putting our love affair on hold, which was turning out to be harder than I'd ever expected, had put us both under a lot more pressure than we realized.

Instead, I concentrated on relaxing for a moment. Away from the chaos of the airport and the fear of traveling to some backwater in pitch black of night, I took in the soothing trade winds. I even seemed to be adjusting to the sickly scent of burning sugarcane dancing on the air. It competed with the more pleasant scent of frangipani flowers – their long, stark branches silhouetted against the night sky, a tuft of umbrella-like leaves topped with a crown of glorious pale white flowers.

A few minutes passed and one of the staff who'd assisted in drumming us into the building arrived with tumblers of iced tea.

Jules woke from his somnolent state, the chink of ice on glass registering somewhere deep in his unconsciousness.

"Anything alcoholic in that?" Frederick mumbled.

I thought he must have been near to detoxing. It had been at least three hours since he'd last been served on the flight.

"No, sir."

Jules looked at me for confirmation.

"It's a nice, iced tea, Jules. You'll enjoy it."

Frederick began fidgeting in his seat. "Don't suppose you can arrange for a couple of nips in mine?"

Our host looked befuddled. I decided to come to his rescue. "Don't take any notice of him. He can sort himself out once he's in his room, or he can head for the bar."

I knew Fred wouldn't hit the bar until he'd dispensed with his duty free. I also knew the roadies would hook up with a local soon enough and score enough drugs to keep them all in a state of total unconsciousness for the duration. For now I needed them all relatively calm and stress free.

His iced tea dispensed with, Jules began to get as agitated as Frederick. "How much longer are we going to have to sit here in the middle of Niagara-fucking-falls?"

"I'm sure it won't be too much longer." I attempted to pacify him. The only thing that would pacify Frederick was already on the way to his room in a duty-free shopping bag.

"Don't they know who I am?"

I smiled and stroked his hand. "No, they don't. That's the point, remember?"

He chewed at his fingernail. "Oh, yeah."

I was dehydrated. I swirled the rapidly melting ice at the bottom of my glass, slurping up the cooling water.

"But we've booked out the whole place. They must think I'm somebody."

I shrugged. "I suppose so."

"Madam-" the Fijian equivalent of a concierge addressed me "-your suite is ready for you now. Our apologies for the delay."

I winked at Jules. "Ooh. Looks like they think I'm the head honcho for this trip."

He bowed his head toward me. "I defer to your greatness." Then he looked up and smiled. A warmth spread through me that had nothing to do with the tropical atmosphere.

"Please follow me."

Jules didn't need asking twice.

"Don't worry about us, ma'am, we'll find our own way." Even after all these hours, Dan couldn't resist taking the piss. I gave him the royal wave, enjoying being the center of attention.

The balance of the crew were being assigned other members of staff. Tired musicians, dancers and roadies were to be avoided at all costs. I was grateful there were no other guests who had to deal with their degenerating state. I'd done my best to preserve the situation, but still I hadn't managed to keep them all away from the bar.

As we climbed the stairs to the second floor, I could see down to the bar area below. The signs were there –bad behavior brewing though Dan was attempting to coral the ring-leaders. I didn't much envy him.

"Let's hope the staff can get them all installed in their rooms before they decide to descend on the locals and cause chaos."

Jules tucked his arm inside mine as we ascended the stairs. "They're just animals."

A strange observation coming from him, I thought.

As we wandered past the internal concrete balconies, I realize all the buildings were built to last around here - big solid concrete structures that could withstand the battering of tropical storms.

"Your suite, madam." Our concierge slid a plastic key into the electronic lock. There was a beep and the door opened.

He then popped the card into a small holder on the

wall by the door. The lights came on and the stunning suite was revealed.

"You must insert the card key here for the lights and the air conditioning to work."

"Fucking great. What happens if you lose your card?"

I sensed Jules was tired and past the point of being reasonable. I manoeuvered him through the entranceway, past the double doors and toward the nearest soft-looking sofa, where he deposited his cynical self.

The décor of the room reminded me of images of an old Singapore - all cane and rattan, with beautiful tiled floors and coarse rugs – though everything was, of course, modern-colonial design classics.

"You just wait here. I'll get the guided tour."

"Whatever." He brushed me aside. His cavalier attitude hurt and I wasn't quite sure why.

I reminded myself that details, unless they related to his show and stage craft, weren't his thing.

By the time I'd finished with the guided tour, our luggage was sitting neatly in the entranceway and Jules was a passed-out mess on the couch. He could sleep anywhere, one of the few benefits of being on the road for years.

He'd curled in a fetal position, his arms tucked tightly into his chest, hands clasped under his chin and knees pulled up. I just stood there. Watching him. I realize I spent far too much time watching him. I also knew I wanted him. Who was I kidding thinking we could come here, to this place and not continue to be lovers?

"Come on, you." I shook his shoulder. The ripple of motion ran through his tightly sprung core, the aftershocks finishing in his feet.

"Noo, Mags, go 'way."

His protests fell on ears that refused to hear. He reminded me again of that twelve-year-old, too tired to get out of the car after a long trip home from an exhausting day of family fun.

"Come on," I coaxed. Of all the methods I'd used over the years, tenderness served me best when he was like this.

"Too tired."

"I know, but you need to get into bed."

He groaned, then sat himself up. He still refused to open his eyes. Sitting there like a groggy fledgling, waiting on its first excursion from the nest.

I dragged him to his feet and he staggered, as if sleepwalking through the gilded cage of our suite. I directed him as if he were on autopilot, toward his room where I poured him onto his bed – which was large enough for the Fijian rugby team to be training on.

Blindly, he pulled his shirt over his head and off, dropping it in a small heap by his side. "God, Mags what time is it?"

"I don't know, but it's time to be sleeping."

The shoes were next, kicked off, with the jeans following swiftly after.

He groped for the covers, somehow having a built-in sense of hotel bed-making techniques, and was cocooned in the crisp white linen in moments.

"Don't close the door, Mags."

"I won't. I'm just next door – okay?"

But he was asleep again, I could tell by the rhythmic rise and fall of his chest.

I turned to leave, but wanted to stay. *No-one will know*. I could climb in beside him and we'd wake up together in the morning.

We were attempting, as far as the world sees, to keep things the way they have always been. I slept in my room, he slept in his room. We spent time together when no one else was around, which wasn't often when we were on tour.

I now knew what purgatory is. I was living it. Stuck between two worlds. Trapped between two lives. We feared that the papers would get hold of the details of our affair. I feared Nick will fall into a deep hole of depression and do something stupid.

We lived in fear.

I wondered continually if anything was worth this.

Then I'd look at him, like now asleep in his bed.

And I'd know it was.

My own room was a carbon copy of his. An interconnecting bathroom meant Jules could bellow for me and I would hear him. In the last few days, before we got here, he'd taken to sleeping with his door open - keeping me near, yet also at arm's length. He now hated being alone.

I unpacked – it didn't take long; I traveled light these days. I needed order around me, a symptom of the constant chaos and chaotic people I worked with.

Clothing and shoes stowed, I took a moment on the balcony. The sickly-sweet combination of scented flowers and roasting sugarcane had been replaced by the salty fragrance of the sea.

I could hear the waves lapping at the beach below me, the rustle of the sea breeze through coconut-palm leaves, and the distant laughter of a crowd enjoying the cooler night air.

A sense of peacefulness stole over me. I needed this break. Living in a fishbowl, under the microscopic gaze of the press and public, was taking more out of me this tour than it ever had before.

I thought again about Jules' soft-ball theory. The hit of a single, soft ball doesn't hurt, but after thousands and thousands of balls you feel hammered by the onslaught.

I tipped my face up to the night where a glorious glittering blanket of stars smattered the sky. The Milky Way stood proud in all of its unpolluted glory. Closing my eyes, I felt at peace, a tiny little speck of dust on the planet, but at one with the vast universe above me.

I was happy to be here.

"That was the best night's sleep I've had in months," Jules said.

I had woken and wandered out to the balcony to look at the beach in daylight, only to find Jules lounging in the recliner. His hair mussed from sleep and early morning stubble across his cheeks, it took all my self-restraint not to climb on top of him and take him, there on the balcony.

"Isn't it to die for?" I sighed, turning my attention to the vista below us.

The beach lay out before us now, a picture-postcard-perfect tropical view. Golden sand, blue water and tall coconut palms. Numerous, thatched umbrellas lined the edge of the yellow ribbon of sand, green hammocks swinging lazily between coconut-palm trunks.

"Yeah, I suppose it's okay."

"Don't knock yourself out with enthusiasm." I felt the

weight of his pessimism lying heavy in the air.

"It's a beach, Mags, just a beach."

"Well, it's a stunningly beautiful beach and I'm going to make sure I go down and enjoy it."

I made my way to the well-appointed kitchen, figuring I'd have a cup of coffee before I went for a swim. I had to do something to burn off the lustful feelings.

Coffee machines spoke no languages. In whichever country you visited, they just were. Here, we had a fine-looking, stainless, automatic-espresso appliance. I turned it on, selected a flat white and waited for the steaming frothy brew to create itself.

Magic!

"Is there such a thing as a newspaper in this third-world backwater?"

"I don't know. I suppose you could check out the front." I poked my head around the balcony window. "You want a coffee?"

"Is it decent? You know I won't drink that instant shit." He was on his feet already, presumably on his way to look for the paper.

"It is."

"Yup, I'll have one."

I heard the front door slam as I removed my frothy brew from the machine's stainless footplate.

Depressing the long-black button, I waited for Jules' coffee to prepare itself.

Hearing the door open again, I asked, "Well, is there news here?"

"There is." He came into the kitchen looking triumphant. "And I don't seem to be a single part of it!"

"See? I told you." I felt smug. "You're a nobody here."

"And that's the way I like it."

He picked me up, twirled me around the kitchen and dropped me back in my spot in front of the coffee machine.

"So..." His voice dropped an octave. I was acutely aware of the lack of distance between us. I could feel the warmth of his body not far from my own, his pungent scent competing with that of the brewing coffee. "Are we going to spend a little time getting to know each other better over this holiday?"

He traced his index finger along my hairline, his hand coming to a stop on my shoulder, thumb resting comfortably in the shallow groove by my collarbone.

A shiver ran through me.

I glanced up at him. My desire to strip him and have my way with him, fighting with my resolve to keep things cool. "We might. If you can behave and we can agree to take it slowly."

His lips brushed the top of my head. "If we took it any more slowly we'd be in reverse."

"Look, Jules, I just don't want any more shit in the newspapers, or on the net. I can't be a part of all that."

"I know, I know." He held me close.

The warming presence of the bulk of his body quieted the racing in my mind.

"It's just all so complicated." I buried my head in the soothing warmth of his breast. I could feel his heart beating, thrumming a steady pace beneath the light cotton of his T-shirt.

He whispered pacifying words to me through my hair; they ran like warm treacle down the long strands, taking eventual residence in the small caves of my ears. "No one knows us here - you told me that. I'm not on the front pages of the papers, or even on the fourth or fifth page. I'm anonymous here. We can just be."

"But the band, the crew?"

"What goes on tour stays on tour. You know that."

He pushed me away from him so I could look into the deep pools of his sea-green eyes. Thick, dark lashes framed eyes that were full of concern. A concern I'd seldom seen for me before.

"We can take this as quickly or as slowly as you like." His eyes never left mine. "You are in complete control here."

"Don't say that." I looked away from him.

His hand, with a sure but gentle touch, turned my face back to his.

I admitted, "It's like leaving the rabbit in charge of the lettuce patch."

He laughed. "I like that."

I broke free from his grip, ostensibly to deal with the coffee sitting on the machine. I feared if I remained close for much longer I'd happily take him back to my bed and make love to him. His words made far too much sense. The temptation of him was far too real.

I handed him his coffee. "Doesn't it bother you that I'm married?"

"Of course it does." He looked hurt. "But I know you don't want to be."

"So you can ignore it."

"Kind of - and Nick walked out on you. Don't forget that."

A bank of gray cloud had rolled in at the northern end of the beach, threatening to blot out the sun's rays. I saw

155

the same blanket of cloud cross Jules' features.

"If I was honest..." He took a sip of his coffee.

I felt myself hanging in the abyss, waiting on the rest of his sentence. "Which I hope you will be," I urged him on.

"I want that nutcase out of your life and you in mine, and I'm prepared to do whatever it takes to achieve that end. Are you prepared to do whatever it takes, Mags?"

It was what I wanted to hear, but it still terrified me - though not enough to turn down his offer. "I am and I will."

"Good girl." He smiled at me, and it instantly washed away my terror. All would be well in my world if I put my faith in this man. Like so many of his followers, I adored him and was prepared to take the risk and do whatever it took to be by his side until the day I died.

CHAPTER THIRTEEN

I wanted us all to wind down. We had a couple of days, so I arranged for us all to go on a tour dinner - the band, the dancers, our close-knit crew and Jules.

The resort sat within a small island of hotels, all serviced by a bula bus - a 1970s single-decker fitted out with grass skirt and thatched roof. There were a number of them doing a circuit of all the hotels day and night, picking up and dropping off guests. It meant we could visit all the other resorts if we felt so inclined, and we didn't have to wear ourselves out walking in the heat of the day.

In the cool of the night, the bula bus transported most of our drunk and/or drugged team from one side of the island to the other without us losing anyone in the swamp or sea. For this trip there were too many of us for one bus, so we split into two groups and agreed to meet at a restaurant four hotels along from our own. It was another semi-exclusive affair since I'd booked out the restaurant for the night, ensuring there would be little chance of us being disturbed - or disturbing any other holidaymakers.

It had always been my experience that in a discreet island such as this one there was little chance of anyone bothering or harassing Jules, but I always erred on the side of caution whenever I exposed us to the public eye.

Otis had gone ahead earlier in the day and given his okay. Not that I thought this was necessary, but I'd been overruled by Jules.

"You know I hate these team-bonding sessions." Jules sat next to me on the bula bus, fidgeting with the end of his T-shirt. He always fidgeted when he was agitated, which seemed to be quite often since we'd been away from the tour.

"Well, we only have to have one of them and you know how valuable Dan thinks they are." I stroked the top of his hand, trying to placate him.

"I don't see the value in sitting around with people I spend days with on tour, just so that they can get pissed and stoned and play up. It's no fun at all."

"Not for you, no. But it's good for them."

"And it's not that I'm a wowser, either."

"I know you're not." Jules had a mistaken idea most people thought less of him when they discovered he didn't partake in drink or drugs.

The media simply assumed Jules' outrageous behavior was attributed to drug taking. We gave up a long time ago trying to tell them that simply wasn't the case, so we allowed the press to write their crappy stories about drug-fueled sex binges.

Dan believed the public needed to think Julian was a recreational drug-user; otherwise he'd be labeled a Christian. I had my doubts and didn't think that would be such a bad thing, but the press had the final word and we

158

were certainly never offered a spot at any Christian festivals.

His public believed what they wanted to believe. It was as it had always been. No amount of PR or denials would change their minds.

Our bula bus pulled into the hotel reception area. The evening air lapped warm at my face and a sense of peace stole over me. Despite Jules' reluctance to be out with the crew, I enjoyed these nights - something interesting always came out of them.

The seventeen or so of us who'd managed to make it into the first bus disembarked. Torches lit the path into the resort reception. A darkly stained wooden footpath stretched out before us. It had the appearance of a long low bridge, with a large expanse of clear water running either side and reminded of a runway scene from an episode of *America's Next Top Model*. I had visions of Tyra Banks and rake-thin models looming toward me at any moment.

We clip-clopped across the almost black wood, which wore its pockmarks with pride - many a stiletto-heeled woman had been before us – and entered an ornate foyer resembling an old-style Singaporean colonial mansion.

Rattan chairs with thick gold-and-cream cushions adorned the room. Huge palms stood in the corners as if they'd presided over the view for centuries. I knew they'd only been here a couple of years, but the illusion of stately grandeur in the heart of the Pacific prevailed.

Our troupe turned left at the entrance to the pool complex and headed toward a gravel pathway marked with illuminated rocks and more flaming torches. A miniature waterfall fell to our right and I could hear the laughter and chatter of children splashing through the other side, along with the sound of parents trying to control an unruly mob.

The air swam thick with the sweet, pungent scent of Pacific frangipani. Staff wore the small yellow or pink flowers in their hair. Spent blooms lay like thick cerise and gold confetti on the sand before us. The whole complex had an air of fantasy about it. I couldn't think of a more romantic place to be in the world with Jules, the only complication being the twenty-eight extras here with us.

"It's beautiful, isn't it?" I snuggled close to Jules, hoping he would feel the magic in the air.

"It's all right. I wouldn't write home about it."

His negative attitude almost crushed my mood. I tried to remind myself he was strung out being around so many people he didn't like it and was just grumpy. Nevertheless, his indifference took the edge off of the magic. I wanted to give him a good slapping for being so ungrateful.

I stopped him for a moment, allowing the crowd to pass us by and move on to the restaurant beyond.

"It's beautiful, Jules. How can you not be moved by a place like this?"

He shrugged, a flat, expressionless look on his face.

"Come on." I could feel my serenity slipping away. "Don't be like this."

"Like what?"

"You know exactly like what." I struggled to stay composed. "I'm supposed to be on holiday as well. I'm here with you. Just you. Remember? And I don't want to be with you when you're behaving like this."

Now he whined, "But you know I hate these things."

160

"Well, you're just going to have to be an adult and think of someone other than yourself for a moment and be a charming host."

"I can't."

"You do it every night on stage. You do it whenever someone points a camera in your face, and you do it whenever there is a reporter sitting at your table." Anger exploded from me in a torrent. "So you can damn well do it for me and you can do it for those people in there who love and support you."

I stormed off, leaving him standing on the small bridge with the sound of children's laughter following me down the pathway.

I could hear Jules chasing me up the path. His feet crunching in the gravel at a steady pace. "Mags, stop." The crunching became uneven, and it sounded as if he had almost fallen. "Dammit!"

I turned around. He was down on hands and one knee in the gravel.

"Fuck!" He looked up at me, despair painted on his face. "Don't make me beg. I need some help."

I laughed.

"And don't laugh at me."

He hated that, but I couldn't help myself.

He stood up. His sandal had buckled under his foot, tripping him. Blood ran down his leg and chunks of gravel were stuck in the bloody mess his kneecap had become.

"I'm hurt. Please don't laugh."

"I'm sorry." I'd forced him to wear shorts and sandals; he'd done it to please me.

"This wouldn't have happened if I was wearing jeans

and sneakers."

"This wouldn't have happened if you weren't being an asshole."

I located the mini packet of tissues stashed in my evening bag, just as Otis appeared, almost materializing out of the warm tropical air.

"You okay?" Otis' eyes tracked to the blood trickling down Jules' shin.

"Yeah, good mate." Jules waved Otis on.   I knew he wouldn't go too far ahead.

 Some days I felt more like a mother than a lover.

Carefully I picked out stone shrapnel from the flesh of his knee.

"Ouch!"

"Don't be a baby, it doesn't hurt."

"How do you know? It's not your knee."

His swift retort reminded me of the number of times I had fallen over and hurt myself as a child, only to be told by an adult it didn't hurt.

"I'm sorry." I felt remorseful.

"It's okay."   His voice softened and he laid his hand in the curve of my back. "It's not your fault. I was just being a jerk."

"You certainly were."

"You guys okay?"   One of the dancers who'd followed in the second bula bus had caught us up. The balance of the mob split down the middle as they moved around us both, like sheep in a sorting yard.

"We're good, Andre," I assured him. "Nothing to worry about here - I'll have him fixed up in no time. You head along to the restaurant. We won't be too far away."

He ambled off. The dancers were a good crowd, a mix

of six men and six women. Andre led the men, as Sheree led the women. Tall and lean, he wore plenty of leather on stage and pretty much nothing else. Jules attracted a large gay following and Andre's antics meant he received almost as much fan mail as Jules, much to his amusement. Andre was a man's man and as straight as they came. That didn't deter the fans one little bit.

I wiped the blood from Jules knee and shin as best I could, then kissed him on the forehead. "We should probably get that looked at."

"It's a scratch. Don't be silly." He dropped the material of his shorts back over his knee. "I'll wash it off in the swimming pool later."

"You can't do that." I was horrified.

"Just watch me."

We joined the rest of the crew in the restaurant. It was set by another sapphire-colored pool which was lit from below, making it look like a piece of blue marble. Perfect.

The dark silhouette of palm trees stood proud in the glow of the torches that illuminated the edge of the resort.

I could hear the sea lapping at the shore, the restaurant sitting on its own small peninsular betwixt the pool and sea.

The large tables of our tour family, as I often liked to think of them, had split into their working groups. The tables were arranged in a herringbone pattern, as you would for a wedding. The tight eight sat at the top table, but Sheree's absence made us seven tonight. Tables of crew, dancers, musicians and assorted wardrobe assistants, accountants and administrators congregated in front of us in their cozy groups. I knew trying to separate them and

163

make them mix would cause complete chaos - I'd given up trying to do that a long time ago.

The only outsider to join us was Sheree's husband. Jules had a soft spot for Sheree, so he was happy for Jeremy to spend the week with us. I watched Sheree and Jeremy, very much a couple in the middle of the large crowd of singles. Sheree had chosen to sit with the dancers, simply because Jeremy was there. He would have been most welcome at the table with us, but she insisted. I knew it had everything to do with Jeremy witnessing the growing relationship between Jules and me. I'd been acutely aware of Sheree's attempts to keep Jeremy away from me since we'd been here.

"How come Sheree's sitting over there with him?" It seemed Jules had been reading my thoughts. Scary.

"Because he's her husband."

"They normally sit up here." Jules seemed peeved.

"She doesn't want him knowing about us. You know what he's like."

"An idiot?" Jules' snarky tone didn't go unnoticed.

I slid my hand under the table and squeezed his upper thigh.

"Don't stop, I like it."

"Not in front of the kids, Jules. Now just behave."

I looked again at Jules and immediately wanted to misbehave.

"No, seriously though. She's not really avoiding us, is she?" Hurt fought with confusion on his features.

"Sometimes you can be so slow. Of course she's avoiding us." I kept my words quiet. I didn't want anyone else overhearing the conversation.

"But that's stupid."

"No it's not, Jules, and this isn't the time or place to discuss it."

The waiter arrived with the first course, cutting short our conversation. A wonderful dish of raw fish in coconut milk, served inside a coconut shell, with a bright-pink hibiscus flower adorning the side of the plate.

The meal passed without incident until an openly gay waiter started making overtures to Jules.

I'd been struggling enough with his female fans. Now this.

"Go on," he whispered by the side of Jules head, loud enough for me to overhear. "You know you've wanted to touch me all night. I can see it in your eyes."

My stomach turned. Grave fears the raw fish might make an unscheduled exit from my tummy crossed my mind. I thought of Young Elvis and remembered why I'd wanted to leave the tour. Why wasn't Jules just giving him the brush-off?

Well then, I would. "He's with me." I smiled my sweetest smile and enjoyed stamping my ownership on Jules.

I didn't like the way he kept leering at me as well.

Sure enough, he tried a different tack. "I'm happy to touch both of you at the same time, if you prefer that idea."

The thought of him touching either of us serially pissed me off and I couldn't keep my mouth shut. "What I want is for you to fuck off and leave us alone."

The pesky waiter minced on his way and Jules looked at me, his eyes full of concern.

"What's the matter with you? He was only having a bit of fun."

"Well, he's not having fun with me. I don't like his attitude."

I struggled to hide my irritation - not only at the waiter, but at my own conflicting feelings around Jules' sexuality. Gay men hadn't bothered me until Young Elvis put in an appearance.

"You're not back on the same bandwagon as the press, are you?"

I shook my head. How could I be mad at Jules? It wasn't his fault the public always wanted a piece of him. I only had to look at his face to see how much my reaction disturbed him.

"Don't lie to me."

"Well, if you know what I'm thinking why did you bother asking?" I spat the words out under my breath. I didn't want the rest of the crew to know that we were arguing - again.

"How many times do I have to reassure you I don't do men?"

"Well, I still don't understand why that Elvis-bloke was in your room then." None of the Young Elvis incident made any sense to me. "You still haven't explained yourself."

"Look-" Jules rubbed the heel of his hand into his eye "- I don't quiz you about what you and your husband got up to in the bedroom. Give me the same courtesy."

I didn't like the way he emphasized the words *your husband*. "I don't want to talk about Nick with you."

"So show me the same consideration and stop bringing up my past."

The objectionable waiter arrived with the main course. He took great care with Jules' meal, but he might as well

166

have thrown mine from the other side of the room. A small rack of lamb that I had been quite looking forward to sat in front of me. My appetite gone, I pushed the food further away from me.

"Don't start with the I'm-not-eating pantomime either." Jules' irritation matched my own.

"Don't tell me what to do." Everything continued to be about him.

"Someone has to look after you. You seem incapable lately of looking after yourself."

"Strange how that's happened since I've been spending more time with you."

Jules pulled the meal back toward me. I wanted to hurl it and him across the room.

He took a deep breath and visibly composed himself. "Let's not do this here. Please."

Bless him. I nearly fell off my chair. "I'll try."

Anger and frustration continued at a low boil below my beltline. I needed a distraction. Who could I call on?

I knew Fred would be missing being on tour. A workaholic musical dynamo, he always hated down time, and getting him along to one of these functions was like herding goldfish with a straw.

However he could always be relied upon to break the tension in a room. He sat not more than a couple of people away from me, on the other side of Dan, wearing an expression of contained boredom. I knew it wouldn't take much for him to become the center of attention. With any luck he and Dan could do a double act, giving me a chance to haul my emotions back under control.

I called across Jules, my hand falling to the top of his thigh, the place where the waiter's had been hovering just a few moments beforehand. I forced that thought out of my mind and plowed on with my plan of distraction.

"Hey, Fred, how's it going?"

Fred looked at me as if I'd gone insane. "You know how it's going. How it always goes when we're not on tour. It sucks."

In a previous life Fred had spent over a decade running music stores with Dan, who'd hired Fred because the man also happened to be one of the best guitar players in the country. Until then Jules had preferred to write songs by himself, but once Fred came on board they'd struck up what had become one of the most outstanding creative relationships in history.

"Why don't you tell the assembled about your days in the music business with Dan?"

Fred took the bait and ran with it. "You remember that time we opened that new store on Main?"

"Remember?" Dan rolled his eyes. "How the hell could I ever forget it!"

"Forget what?" I pricked up my ears. Comic relief would be a bonus about now.

I cast a quick glance across toward Sheree and Jeremy. Sheree was looking lovingly in Jeremy's direction but Jeremy's eyes were on me. Steel-cold and hard. Had he been watching us? I suspected he had and my stomach went back into knotted spasm all over again.

I decided to brazen it out and held direct eye contact with him and then smiled. I wanted to look my most charming.

Jeremy's expression didn't change. Sheree's eyes followed his gaze across the room and she returned my cheery smile with a warm and happy one of her own. I couldn't believe it. Could she be so in love - or in love with the idea of being in love - she was oblivious to his moods?

Sheree touched the side of Jeremy's face in such a tender way, watching the exchange made me ache. With great reluctance Jeremy turned his attention back to his wife but then his expression immediately changed. A warmth spread across his features, evening them out. It was impossible not to see how in love they both were.

Did Jules and I share a love for all the world to see? If so, it would be impossible for us to hide our love from the world.

I cast the disturbing thought from my mind and turned my attention back to Frederick who, as if on cue, took center stage, rolling up the cuffs of his shirt and preparing to tell us a tale I knew would have us all in hysterics.

A lingering feeling of darkness pervaded my world, creeping in at the edges. I couldn't shake an unprecedented feeling of impending doom.

"Well, we'd spent weeks fitting out the shop. It was beautiful. All black and chrome, the lighting nearly in place. We were due to open in a couple of days but I couldn't get the phones on."

Dan interjected - he loved to assist in the theatrical telling of Fred's stories. "Yeah, it was impossible to get a phone line on in less than three weeks in those days."

A shout came from the crowd. "The dark ages, you mean?" Everyone loved to tease the boys about their age.

"Piss off." Dan looked huffy. He didn't like to be reminded that he was nearer to sixty than forty. His years in the industry stood us all in good stead, but secretly he still wanted to be Jules' age.

"Anyway-" Fred continued with the story "-we

169

eventually got a phone technician in the place, but it got to the end of the day and still no phones."

Dan doubled over laughing. "You won't believe what he did." He pointed his finger at Fred, nearly hysterical.

"What did you do?" We were all on the edge of our seats with anticipation. Dan was nearly on the floor, eyes closed, rocking backwards and forwards.

"I nailed the bastard in."

"You *what?*"

"He did." Dan squeaked the words out.

"That's right." Fred had a devilish grin on his face. "Told him he wasn't going bloody anywhere until I had a working phone."

"What d'ya mean, nailed him in?" came the call from the floor.

I put a packing case lid over the doorway and nailed a piece of four by two over it."

Dan was on the floor by now, crying with laughter. "Fred told him he wasn't coming out of there until he'd got the phones going."

"Did it work?" I was incredulous.

"Sure did." Dan managed to clamber weakly onto the nearest chair, tears still streaming down his cheeks.

"What about the opening?" Fred clapped Dan on the back. "You tell that story better than me."

"I can't." Dan was still gasping for air. "You tell 'em."

"Oh, God, not this again." Jules rolled his eyes.

"Stop it. I want to hear." I stroked Jules hand.

His face took on the look of a teenager having to sit through yet another boring history lesson. "But I've heard this before."

"The rest of us haven't, so just be quiet." Sheree gave

Jules one of her famous stares, almost as intense as the one Jeremy had been giving me earlier.

"Lord save me," Jules muttered under his breath.

I jabbed him in the ribs and followed up Sheree's stare with one of my own.

He fidgeted at my side and waited for Dan to begin.

"Well, we decided - didn't we, Fred?" He looked to Fred for approval.

"We did." Fred agreed, nodding his head.

"We decided we'd make this new shop the buzz of the city. We wanted to get as many people there as we could on the opening day, so we thought we'd be smart-" Dan jabbed his finger at his temple "-and do something no one else had done."

"You guys? Smart?" Jules huffed.

"Stoppit," I hissed. He was being disagreeable because he wasn't the center of attention. Fred and Dan had the entire room hanging on their every word.

Fred took over the storytelling; he couldn't help himself. "So we took out adverts in all the local papers."

"Full-page ads," Dan interjected. "They cost us a mint."

Fred continued, "We had guitars for a dollar, a drum kit for ten bucks, stuff like that."

"You're kidding?" Ted looked horrified.

"A drummer's dream, Ted, you're right."

"You'd have had every drummer in the city on your doorstep." Ted's eyes glazed over.

"We did. And the rest."

"You remember, we had old Robert Fisk on the door?" Fred spoke exclusively to Dan.

"Yeah, yeah. He had those white gloves, you remember?" Dan became more and more animated as

Fred told the story.

"He did."

"Anyway, we managed to get the phone lines on and we let the technician out of the building. That's when we realized a whole load of people were already beginning to accumulate outside. We were a couple of days out from the opening, but they were setting up camp outside the door, you know?"

"Like they do for my ticket sales?" Jules piped up from beside me.

"Yeah, Jules mate, like they do for you." Dan winked at Fred. "But it was pretty unheard of in those days for anyone to camp outside a store."

"We were ahead of our time in the marketing sense, weren't we?" Fred looked a little wistful for a moment.

"So what happened?" Sheree's legendary impatience began to make itself known.

"It came to opening morning and we were terrified. We'd just spent a fortune fitting out a new shop, it was full of stock, and we had hundreds of people outside." Fred threw his arms wide. "There was no way we could control them."

"Next thing, there's a policeman knocking on the front door." Dan grimaced.

"I stuck my head out the window - there was no fucking way I was going to open the door." Fred knew he had us all now, and was milking it for all it was worth.

Jules had his head in his hands.

"He said, 'Do you gentlemen know there's no police presence in town big enough to control the mob who you've out here?' Of course I said, 'No, officer, I had no idea that was the case."

Dan carried on, "I was out the back just shitting myself."

I knew these two men and the chaos they could manufacture, and I could imagine the scene they were describing.

"My gut told me that as soon as we opened those doors it was just going to be mayhem."

"But you had to, right?" I prompted them on, despite Julian's audible heavy sighing. How they ever got through, I couldn't imagine.

"It was like this," Dan continued. "I realized that what we needed was a huge police presence."

Fred nodded. "But I'd just told him that Mr Plod out the front had washed his hands of us."

"Truly, I know how Christ felt after Herod washed his hands of him. At the mercy of the rabid forces of the public." Dan shuddered.

"Terrifying." Fred mirrored the shudder.

"It's how I feel every night going on stage."

I didn't know whether Jules was empathizing or just trying to turn the focus back to himself.

"Good old Robert Fisk had a bunch of dodgy mates who were part of a motorcycle club."

"You mean gang connections." Jules was really being obtuse now.

"The old copper from out the front had come around the back. He wasn't able to offer us any police protection, but he had a whole load of hats he said we could borrow." Fred looked Dan in the eye. "You remember?"

"Oh, God, how could I forget?"

"You're not serious?" I couldn't believe what I was hearing.

"They are." Jules sounded bored.

I ignored him. "What kind of a police force were they running back then?"

"Not a great one." Dan continued on with the story. "So, we held off the stampeding masses out the front while we arranged for a group of the gang's security guys to arrive and make a circle around the perimeter of the building."

"Don't believe you."

"It's true."

"Mate-" Dan slapped his knees again "-you remember the nutter who was preaching?" The two them were like a Laurel and Hardy comedy tag team.

"The one stood on the barrel with a *Bible* in his hand?" Dan pointed his finger wildly into the air.

"Yeah, that's the one. Kept banging on about how commercialism was the spawn of Satan and we were his emissaries brought from Hell."

The two of them were nearly crying with laughter now. Even Jules had perked up. "You never told me about that before."

"He looked like a Quaker, didn't he?"

"I was expecting to see a horse tethered around the corner, with a carriage attached. Not something you'd see in the Southern hemisphere."

"What happened next?" Sheree was engrossed.

"Well, that was where old Rob Fisk and his white gloves came into the act."

Act? It sounded like a three-ring circus routine. No wonder these two were so at home on tour - their whole lives had been a commercial ringside ride.

"You remember how he put them on?" Fred's full

attention was on Dan. This was obviously something they had recounted many times. No wonder Jules was bored.

So why had I never heard the tale before now?

Dan stood up, taking center stage in the middle of the group. "I was heading to the front door, terrified, but I knew we were going to have to let them in. The racket outside got louder and louder. If we didn't let them in they'd just bust the bloody door down. The security guards-"

"Gang members!" Jules was heckling.

"-were wearing the police hats with their security uniforms and had formed a line in front of the doors. I got to the front door, but then old Rob Fisk put his hand up like this."

Dan held up his hand like a policeman indicating that a car should stop. "You remember, Fred - right in my face."

Fred nodded.

"I remember and I wasn't even there."

The entire engrossed group turned on Jules, telling him to be quiet.

"Then he put those bloody gloves on."   Dan, in pantomime, exaggerated the action of a man putting on gloves, finger by finger. "He walked to the door, unlatched it and threw it open to the screaming mob outside. I braced myself for the onslaught. But again, before a single braying member of the public could make it across the threshold he held up that gloved hand and they all stopped in their tracks."

Dan was giggling again. Fred, in hysterics, had taken Dan's place on the chair, unable to stay on his feet any longer.

Dan went on, "He called them in, one at a time,

signaling with a gloved finger when they could cross the doorstep. The whole boiling cauldron of humanity just stood there and waited to be called into the shop, one by bloody one, by him with the gloved hand."

"No way." Sheree couldn't believe what she was hearing.

Dan was slapping his thigh now. "Absolutely yes way. He was amazing, wasn't he, Fred?"

Fred nodded. "We used him again on some of those early tours we did with the Rockos and Midnight Shame. He was great security. I think it was the gloves - no one was prepared to mess with the gloves."

"Perhaps I should invest in a pair." Otis grinned, lifting a large black eyebrow.

"Mate, you'd look like one of the Black and White Minstrels." Jules was back on form now we'd come to the end of the story.

Otis took to the center of the floor, doing a soft-shoe shuffle with an imaginary top hat and cane.

When he had finished, everyone cheered and applauded, wolf whistles abounding.

To my astonishment, Jules jumped up beside me, as appreciative as everyone else. Taking advantage of my surprise, he pulled me into his arms and kissed me. The roar from the appreciative mob increased in volume as they witnessed the public declaration of our love.

I knew one person who wouldn't be cheering for us — but I was way past caring.

CHAPTER FOURTEEN

The evening seemed to generally degenerate from there.

"Can't we go yet?" Jules shuffled in his seat.

"No." I glared at him. "We can't leave when everyone else is still here having a good time."

"They know we're together." He slid his hand down the side of my thigh. The touch through the sheer fabric of my dress ran up my leg like a shot of electricity.

I looked into his eyes. They shone sea-green back at me. The light in his soul beamed through those portals to the outside world.

"Behave!"

"I don't want to behave - and they're not behaving." He knew he'd win me over with his persistence and charm.

I was under his spell, but like a small mouse fighting valiantly to the death with a hunting cat I stood my ground. "We can't go yet. No one else has."

"They're never going to leave." He continued his pulsating strokes down the side of my thigh. It didn't matter now and anyway - most of them were drunk or stoned out of their tiny minds. "Half the band are out in the men's toilets sniffing coke off the dancers' tits."

"Julian, don't be gross." I hated it when he talked like that.

"It's true. You know what they're like."

I well knew what they were like, and it was the reason he wanted to leave.

"Right, who's in for a jam session?" Fred was high, I could tell. Jules frowned and looked as if he'd rather be out in the ocean, despite the fact that he couldn't swim.

I looked at Dan, who said, "Fred organized this with the resident band before we got down here."

I could see now that a few of the boys had brought their guitars down. The girls were clearing a space to dance.

Jules laid his head on the table, scowling at me. "I'm not going up there."

"You know you will and you'll enjoy yourself."

"Or what?" He ran his hand down my spine, lingering with intricate circular motions in the lower part of my back. "You might punish me later?"

"Punish?" My back ached from sitting all evening. The heat from his hand soothed the ache, as well as warming my libido. "You know I'd never punish you."

"Even if I asked you nicely?" The sparkle in his eye suggested he'd be more than willing.

My libido ratcheted up another notch. Maybe we should be leaving.

"Jules!" Frederick's yell from the stage competed with the sounds of a Western drummer acquainting himself with Fijian drums. I knew we were in for a treat, even if Jules seemed keener to be heading back to the suite.

"You have to go." I smiled sweetly at him.

He pinched the small of my back and made to get up.

"This had better be worth it."

I knew it would be, and settled back to enjoy the impromptu show.

The combination of European-style jamming with a taint of fresh Fijian village sound made for an interesting session. Some of Jules' numbers were given a makeover and the results varied from hilarious to amazingly melodic. The highlight of the evening had to be Fred falling across the stage in hysterics, almost unable to continue playing, as Jules imitated a Fijian dancing girl while singing the lyrics of his latest number one song.

A group of local girls were showing our dancers how to perform traditional Fijian dances. Sheree and her girls danced in the confined space they'd created in the restaurant, trying new moves that I knew would eventually work their way into a future show. The table and kitchen staff abandoned their posts and came out to join us all. It had become one great big brawling party.

I watched Jeremy watching Sheree, grateful he'd ceased staring at me and Jules, but disturbed by his seeming lack of ability to join his wife and her girls.

A nagging sense of distrust had begun to build between me and Jeremy. I shook myself, dismissing the pessimistic thoughts and concentrating on the deteriorating scene before me.

"Mags, get down here!" Shez motioned from the middle of the crowd.

"Yeah, come on, Mags." Jules' voice cut in across the PA. I found the entire room gesturing for me to join the writhing mass of sweating humanity.

Putting aside my negative thoughts, I left the table and

grabbed Dan by the arm.

"Oy. Leave me be." He struggled to detach himself from my rigid grip.

"If I have to get out there, then so do you." I dragged him reluctantly from his seat. He seemed a little unsteady on his feet - more I hoped due to the number of empty booze bottles on the table, not his increasing age. We made our way to the middle of the floor and started dancing.

Jules blew me a kiss across the throng. Again the crowd erupted, applauding and wolf-whistling their approval.

I could feel the heat moving to my face. Dan grinned at me. I knew Jules and I had their approval.

Instinctively I looked back to where Jeremy sat.

A somber, dark stone.

No approval could be seen etched into his features, only a sharp chord of condemnation. It ran through the crowd like a laser beam, directed at my and Julian's love.

I turned quickly away from the cold, hard stare, concentrating on the love, warmth and appreciation I felt from the swaying bodies surrounding me. I let myself be taken away on the magic carpet of music and surrendered my soul to the God-like figure of Jules.

Hours later, Jules and I made our way back to our rooms.

"You don't like Jeremy much, do you?" His question seemed inappropriate somehow. "It's not like you. What's the matter?

His intuition - or lack thereof - annoyed me. "I don't want to talk about Jeremy."

"Why does he piss you off so much?"

"Because he disapproves of us."

"Lots of people will disapprove of us. You're just going to have to get used to it." He stopped and pulled me to him. I was warm and sticky, a light sheen of sweat making the light cotton of my dress cling to me. "What matters is that I love you." He kissed me on the nose. "And that you love me."

I returned his kiss, on the lips. A deep and significant kiss that sealed forever any doubts I had about being with this man. Whatever the consequences of our union, I knew in the immediacy of the moment there would be no other man for me.

Ever.

I lay next to Jules between the cool sheets, still warm in places from our lovemaking. I felt a sense of contentedness and serenity that had been missing from my life for a long time.

The light from the moon, hung in a cloudless southwest Pacific sky, shone like a torch light through the open windows. I hated air-conditioning so, much to Jules' annoyance, we were lying encased within the humid, Island trade winds.

I must have dozed off. When I was woken from a dreamless sleep by Jules, the moon that had previously lit the room was eclipsing.

"Are you okay?" My question hung amid the eerie half-light of the room.

"The lightning woke me." Jules' words seemed to cling to the static which filled the space between us. He walked out to the balcony and sat down on a small wicker lounger.

I got up, padding after him, no thought to either of our nakedness. Clothes were something Jules put on for a show, and any inhibitions I'd been harboring about my body had been washed away by his total acceptance of me.

Lightning from an approaching electrical storm cracked across the blackened sky. I hadn't seen anything like it – the strange and unnatural sight of the moon being gradually devoured by shadow. I curled myself like a cat inside the cocoon of Jules' naked body.

He leaned over and kissed me.

I woke to the dawn streaking its way across the retreating night sky. I made to escape from the snug security of Jules' sleeping body.

"Where are you going?"

"I thought you were still asleep." Carefully, I peeled my skin from the wicker seat.

Jules ran his fingers over the slight indentations left in my buttocks. "It's like trying to sleep on a rack," he said.

"Perhaps you should go back to bed."

"Are you coming too?" He rubbed an eyebrow with the heel of his hand and he too peeled himself from the lounger.

"No. I'm going for a walk."

"What is it with you and walking at dawn?"

"It's peaceful. And occasionally, I like to greet the day before anyone else does."

"But only when you're on holiday?"

"That's right."

He stumbled back to bed, lying on his back and throwing his arms up above his head. I dressed quietly, admiring the line of his body under the light sheet.

The sharp peak of his hip bone.

The plateau of his belly.

The rise of his ribcage and the dark hair that resided on his chest. It drew me to him, like a moth to a flame. I was incapable of walking past his bare chest without touching him.

I nuzzled my face into the comforting hair, breathing in his scent.

He moaned. "Thought you were going for a walk."

"You know I can't resist you."

He chuckled, the sound reverberating through the dense mass of his chest. I felt his hand creep down the cheeks of my buttocks, forcing my panties to my knees.

I kicked them off and removed my light sundress at the same time.

I slipped under the sheet beside him as he collected my body and almost instantly slid his hard cock inside of me.

A sigh escaped my lips. He filled me.

"What happened to the walk?" Jules asked.

"It can wait."

The party had obviously made its way back to our resort at some stage after Jules and I left.

"Come to check the devastation?" Dan sat on one of the only pool chairs still surviving; most of the balance were sunk at the bottom of the hotel pool. Cigarette butts, bottles and smashed glass littered the entire area.

I surveyed the scene. "How much is this little lot going to cost?" The morning destruction telling the tale of the night's drunken rousting. A prostrate staff member lay on the only other lounger left on dry land and under a frangipani tree I could make out the faint shape of a person curled in the fetal position.

Dan shrugged. He had a bottle of local water by his side, which he took a swig from.

"You look awful. You haven't even been to bed, have you?"

His eyes were bloodshot, his shirt torn and he appeared to have lost his shoes.

"I managed to contain the mayhem to here, at least." He coughed, and then proceeded to light a cigarette.

"Since when did you start on the cancer sticks again?"

"I only smoke when I drink, you know that." He took a huge drag on the cigarette.

It was a habit I was glad I'd missed. I had enough demons to deal with.

Blue smoke snaked from his nostrils as he told me about their early morning exploits. "It all went to hell after you and Jules left."

That's why we went, I thought.

"Your mate, Jeremy, decided it was time for Shez to go, but she wasn't in the mood for that."

"I can imagine." I poked Dan in the arm. His flesh felt spongy, the muscle soft, and I remembered how much older he was than the rest of us, how hard life on tour must be for him. "And he's not my friend."

Dan coughed again, a wheezing, hacking, morning-smoker's cough. The body under the frangipani tree moved in response to the sound, but then settled back into its earthen bed.

"After we'd all been back here a while, a bunch of the lads decided they were going to take the bus to another resort."

"Oh, shit."

"Don't worry." Dan smiled. "Me and the management - those who weren't partying with us - threw them off the bus and kept them here."

"Well done." The trick with out-of-control musicians is to contain them. "So this is the only collateral damage then?"

He nodded, taking a final drag on the cigarette before pitching the butt in the pool to float with the others.

"Ugh." I couldn't contain my revulsion at the sight of the debris floating in the once pristine pool.

"That is unless you count Jeremy going feral on us and punching out half the crew."

"He's a problem. He really shouldn't be here." I thought again about the looks he'd directed at me last night and shuddered.

"But if Jules wants Shez on board, Jeremy's going to have to be a part of the family." Dan's face contorted as his hungover mind contemplated the problems going forward.

"So what happened?" Looking around I could imagine. I don't know why I bothered to ask.

"A bit too much sensual dancing for his liking." Dan looked up at me, shading his bloodshot eyes from the sun, its rapid arrival over my left shoulder heating the area to boiling point. "Too many lads getting too close to his girl."

I shook my head, "She just doesn't get it, does she?"

Dan nodded. "No she doesn't."

He made to stand up, a little unsteady on his feet. "Anyway, I shipped them both off to their room. I doubt we'll see much of anyone for a while."

"And this mess?" The stench of stale alcohol and

cigarettes began to rise with the heat.

"Sorted with the management." Dan hitched up his light cotton trousers. I could see bloodstains on them from the fight. I wondered what state the rest of the group were in. "But they don't want a repeat performance."

"Don't worry, they won't be getting one."

I mentally calculated how many more nights we had here. Whale spotting with Jules today, cameras in tow – though the crew were likely to be thin on the ground. I'd have to check to see who was well enough to survive the boat trip.

The boat trip.

My stomach lurched and it wasn't due to hunger. But we were out of here tomorrow, and tonight the non-boaties would all be too sick for a repeat performance.

"It's a good job breakfast isn't your favorite meal of the day." Dan tossed the comment over his shoulder, like one of the many pieces of litter that sat at my feet.

I headed for the restaurant, wondering what else was going to greet me.

The furniture had all been pushed to one side of the room, presumably to make space for dancing. Meals had been ordered and devoured and debris and wreckage still lay strewn across the tables.

There was no movement anywhere except for a small black cat, who with carefully placed white paws picked its way across the refuse-laden tables, stopping occasionally to sniff at remains.

"Holy shit! The band strikes again." At the sound of Jules' voice the cat made a run for it, in its haste sending a serving dish and several pieces of cutlery clattering to the wooden floor.

"I thought you were sleeping." I reached up to kiss the stubble-covered hollow under his chin.

He nuzzled down into my lips. "I felt like something to eat." He grinned widely. "Other than you."

"Well, you're not going to get anything here."

"That I can plainly see."

"How about we go and visit another resort, before we hit the tide and do some whale spotting?"

He'd remembered. This wasn't the Jules I knew.

"You thought I'd forgotten why we're here, didn't you?"

I nodded.

"Well, I haven't. So let's get this show on the road."

We boarded the wide catamaran, its thrumming twin engines reminding me more of my local launderette than the clean and green Pacific.

Climbing the gangplank, I held onto the steel railing so hard, my knuckles went white. My fear of heights surfaced, and the moving deck reminded me of the rock-climbing incident with Jules.

He'd shared with me his fear of going on stage and yet it didn't stop him facing his fear night after night. I remained in awe of Jules' ability to hold a crowd at his fingertips. What was it about him that enabled him to sway 80,000 people? The comforting presence of his hand at my back reminded me: he made every single one of them feel special and safe and touched by only him. In spite of his own fear of the water, Jules showed his concern for me, making sure I traversed the thin plank with ease.

It disturbed me to discover that two of the few people who were able to make the trip today were Shez and

Jeremy. Considering the reports I'd heard about Jeremy taking out half the crew the night before, he looked alarmingly well and free of bruises. Sheree, on the other hand, seemed on the cusp of not being able to get on the boat.

"I feel like shit," she whispered to me in conspiring tones.

"Then why are you here?" I hissed back, wishing they'd both stayed in bed.

I smiled for the camera crew we'd paid to follow us for the day.

"Because I'd never hear the end of it from Jeremy." Sheree repositioned her oversize sunglasses on her pale face, trying in vain to escape the harsh southern sunlight.

"You know he can't keep coming if he's going to be surly as hell and beat everyone up."

"You can talk. From what I heard, Nick decked Dan before heading off into the wild blue yonder - and, watching you and Jules around each other lately, I can understand why."

"Actually, it was the other way round - Dan decked Nick." Nevertheless, her words stung.

Jules chose that exact moment to slip his arm around my waist. I moved instinctively away from him. Hurt and confusion registered on his face.

"I need to talk to the film crew." It was a pathetic excuse to remove myself from the difficult situation.

"What about?" Jules tried to follow me.

"You stay there." I needed to get away from Sheree; talk of Nick still disturbed me.

Jeremy continued to circle on the outside of the small group. He reminded me of a shark, waiting for the first

188

spill of blood before the feeding frenzy.

I shuddered and made my way toward the cameraman and his sound assistant.

"So, where are the whales we're supposed to be saving?" Jules addressed Dan directly.

"They migrate up here past the outer coral reefs on their way to their breeding grounds."

"You don't see many whaling boats out there though, do you?" I asked. I couldn't imagine anything more revolting than murdering whales. "What species are we looking for today?"

"I don't think that the species really makes any difference at all." Dan looked bemused. "It's just about whether or not we can get the kind of publicity we need."

"Hopefully I've dealt with that," I said, almost to myself. I still had my doubts about whether or not this was a good idea.

"The record company is more interested in me writing decent songs, not whether I can save whales from exploitation." I knew Jules loved the romance of conservation, but being out on the ocean in a boat didn't bring him on.

"They just want bums on seats." I was beginning to sound like Dan.

"Controversy gets bums on seats." Dan winked at me. I gave him the *don't-you-dare* stare.

"The tour's booked solid after this break, isn't it?" Fred's genuine enquiry broke the tension between Dan and me.

"It wasn't but it is now."

"Why do I need to bother chasing whales then?" Jules

looked increasingly uncomfortable aboard the boat.

"I thought you'd enjoy the whale watching." I squeezed Jules hand, knowing he was putting on a brave face. He tickled the inside of my palm in response.

"I'll try, just for you." A smile touched the edge of his lips. "But I don't want a posse of press watching me."

I laughed. "That won't happen. Just the cameraman and his sound guy over there. Then we're going to feed them out through the usual PR channels. You're a nobody here, you keep forgetting that."

"Oh, yes, my son," Dan chimed in. "Nothing as unpredictable as allowing a team of paparazzi to follow you in a dinghy.

"If we did invite them, maybe a whale would tip them out and they'd drown."

"Karma, Jules, karma," I scolded. "Don't put that kind of attitude out there."

"But it'd solve a few of our problems if a boatload of them vanished off the planet."

"Fred, don't you start." I wagged my finger at him and the rest of the crew laughed at us.

"Besides, Fred and I have written some cracker stuff while we've been on tour, haven't we, Fred?"

Fred nodded. Sometimes I couldn't keep up with where Jules' mind went. I could have been forgiven for thinking he had ADHD.

"What does song writing have to do with whale watching?" I asked, bemused.

Jules shrugged. "We're still on tour, aren't we? Fred and I never stop working."

The tour. I'd almost forgotten about the tour as we chased non-existent whales in the middle of the Pacific. I

Private Love in a Public Place

wondered some days, how did I get here?

CHAPTER FIFTEEN

I'd succeeded in avoiding Jeremy for most of the morning and remaining calm amid the rolling waves. Sheree had, no surprise, been seasick and he attended to her every queasy need. Sheree's vomiting episodes were a great reason to stay away from her, and thus magically avoid the ever-present and penetrating stares of the judgmental Jeremy.

"You know that whales arrive every year to mate and calve in these waters, don't you?" Jules said. Hours in front of the television were paying off.

Ted pretended to look interested. I knew he really didn't give a toss. He was here because he loved Jules, and like most of the band would do anything for him.

I'd reminded Jules he had to quit with the touchy-feely routine with me and concentrate on putting together a convincing campaign for the whales. He appeared to have taken me at my word and was sounding every inch the Discovery channel expert for the camera crew, who continued to tail him like paparazzi.

"It's mainly the South Pacific humpback whales that

head this way, but we might catch sight of some killer whales or bottlenose and spinner dolphins..."

Ted continued to feign interest. Otis and Verne, on the other hand - satisfied their precious cargo was safe whilst aboard the vessel - were enjoying the education and hanging on every whaley word.

"So how big are these whales anyways?" Otis' enthusiasm washed across the deck at the same moment I caught an eyeful of spray coming over the bow.

The vastness of the open ocean concerned me. It seemed to stretch into the distance no matter which way I looked. Turquoise waves dipped and then rose into impossible, frothy peaks, reminding me of foamed milk from the countless cappuccinos I'd consumed on tour.

The boat, seeming to have a mind of its own, pitched again, and the sea's spray was collected by the wind and driven into my salt-laden eyes. I felt as if I'd swum the entire distance.

Jules addressed Otis' question. "The humpbacks can get up to 14.5 meters long..."

"What's that in feet?" Verne had yet to become acquainted with European metric measurements.

"Uh...." Jules looked at me.

"Big," I suggested helpfully.

"I think you multiply it by three, don't you?" Ted had never struck me as any kind of a mathematician.

I had no idea and couldn't do the mental arithmetic anyway.

"That makes it nearly forty feet," Jules marveled, and as if on cue a humpback broke the surface of the water, flicking a huge flipper into the air.

I forgot about my fear of the expanse of water and

goggled at the sight in front of me.

"See. See. See." Jules' enthusiasm was contagious. "They can weigh 40 tonnes and their flippers can be five meters long. The song they sing is their mating song. They say it's rather complex."

A bit like his lyrics some days, I thought.

He sounded like a compere at Sea World, though another machine-gun volley of spray in my eyes reminded me we were far from the safety of a stand in Sea World. The captain slowed the catamaran and we began to rock precariously, the boat tipping as a large swell hit us and then sliding gracefully down the other side of the rolling water.

I heard Sheree moan and was grateful for the advice given to me earlier in the day to keep my eyes on the horizon.

"Look!" In his excitement Jules had embraced me, maneuvering me to the bow of the boat where the tips of the two large hulls alternately dipped and then glided high on either side of us.

The humpback flung itself out of the water, almost standing on its tail before smashing back into the ocean. I was stunned.

"Can you imagine the sheer power?" Jules wondered, and I had to agree. How could you not be caught up in the grandeur and might before us?

"It's astonishing." I couldn't imagine how whalers could kill something as amazing as the creature putting on this dazzling display.

Jules arm remained tight around me, protectively holding me despite the swirling sea.

I looked up at him and said, "I'm glad Dan brought us

here." The sparkle in his eyes, the sheer splendor and beauty of our aquatic surrounds and my sense of being exactly where I should be at this moment filled me with a sense of peace and calm.

Waves crashed, people screamed, and as the wind whipped up the rolling sea it felt as if we were a tiny cork bobbing in a washing machine.

Jules looked down, caught my eye and then kissed me.

Long.

Slow.

Hard.

"You two are pathetic!" As Jeremy helped a still pale and feeble Sheree off the boat he spat the comment in our direction with the venom of a snake paralyzing its prey.

"Leave them alone - they're in love." Sheree came to our rescue, while Jules and I stood reeling.

"You shouldn't defend them." Jeremy turned on Sheree.

"Leave her alone." Jules came to his senses and took a couple of purposeful paces toward the other man.

"Don't you tell me what to do, you piece of shit!" Jeremy snarled, but at Jules' advance took a small step backwards, the movement upsetting the balance he and Sheree had on the narrow gangplank. Sheree stumbled, lurching in Jules' direction, but he managed to catch her before she hit the wooden jetty.

"Take your fucking hands off my wife!" Jeremy's enraged voice caught the attention of the cameraman, who started filming the fast deteriorating disembarking.

I looked at Otis, who nodded and made his way at speed toward the man holding the camera. I didn't want this on film.

"You're not on fucking stage with her now, you pervert." Jeremy was becoming more and more incensed by the moment.

"Mate, just calm down. She was going to hit the deck. You want me to stand here and let that happen?" Jules, bless him, remained calm and in control throughout the onslaught.

"Jeremy, you're making a scene. Stop it." Sheree collected herself and stood up straight, though she still looked as pale as the twin hulls of the gleaming boat moored behind her.

She turned her attention to Jules. "I'm sorry. He's just upset."

"Don't fucking apologize to that perverted piece of shit." I decided Jeremy must be looking for a fight.

Jules took charge. "Look, I can see what you're trying to do here but abusing me isn't going to get her fired. She's my best dancer and the only way she's leaving is if she decides she wants to."

Jeremy's face went a deeper shade of red. Jules had obviously been spot on.

"Jeremy, shut up. I'm sorry, Jules, I don't know what's gotten into him." Sheree disengaged from Jules' hold, wrenched herself free from Jeremy and, with a measure of dignity I didn't know she had, headed for the waiting taxi.

"This isn't over by a long shot." Jeremy spat the toxic words toward us and strode after his wife.

Jules took my arm. I trembled, but this time it had nothing to do with his touch.

Back on tour, on the final leg, we left the chaos of the South Pacific and jealous husbands behind us. The plight of the South Pacific whales had been highlighted, and now one day rolled into another as Jules and the band performed.

The record company came out and publicly dumped Jules, branding him a bisexual, strung-out Greenie hippy.

Jules didn't seem to care.

I carried with me the constant, nagging fear that Jeremy would pop up somewhere, or try to drag Sheree away from the tour. I expected on a daily basis to read something disgusting about us in the press. He'd left Fiji quietly enough - but I knew it wasn't over.

Nick sent me an email. My personal possessions were in a storage unit in London. He'd changed the locks and the security code on the house. He wanted a divorce and I would get nothing.

I stopped eating. At least I could control what went in my mouth.

Jules was beside himself with worry. "Mags, you have got to eat. You're wasting away in front of me."

We were in yet another hotel suite and for a moment I couldn't remember which city we were in, but then I realized we were in Singapore. "I'll be fine. I had breakfast."

"Half an apple and a quart of coffee doesn't count."

He held me in his arms. I'd been avoiding him for so long I'd forgotten how easy I could dissolve into him.

"Jesus, there's nothing to you." He brushed his lips across the crown of my head.

I began to melt, and for a second the tension I carried started to dissipate - like I imagined snow would on the hot concrete outside. "You don't need to worry about me."

"Mags, you're the first person in the world I've ever

cared about. I've been so wrapped up in myself I have no opinion on anything else. I don't know how to have an opinion on anything else."

He kissed me. I could almost taste the desperation on his lips. "You've changed all that."

Disembarking from the closeted and air-conditioned comfort of the jet, on our way to the final show of the tour, I was assaulted by the warmer climate. The rigmarole of international travel had never been one of Jules' strong points so he was fidgety and flighty as we approached immigration. He hated dealing with what he'd previously described as the bureaucratic discretions of small-minded zealots in blue uniforms, and I knew he would be disturbed that he was described as an "alien".

"Jesus, Mags, what do you mean I have to zigzag my way down that moronic alleyway?" We'd been spared the chaos of disembarking with the herds from cattle class, but there was still no avoiding the frustration and indignation of border control.

We were all tired and cranky. "Just do it, Jules, please." A ten-hour flight and my usual patient alter-ego's vanished. I began to imagine how a mother I'd seen traveling alone with four young children must feel. I only had Jules to contend with.

I rummaged around in my hand luggage for our passports and realized I hadn't completed the required documents for entry into the southern-hemisphere haven. "Shit!"

"What's the matter?" Julian danced from foot to foot, furtively checking the approaching hordes who'd now disembarked behind us.

"I haven't filled in the arrival cards."

I grabbed Jules by the back of his hoodie and dragged him back through the accumulating crowd to a plastic white table at the side of the arrival hall.

"Fuck, Mags. Where are my sunglasses?" Jules began to unzip the multitudes of pockets on his satchel while trying desperately to disappear into his cap.

I looked up from my scribbling, wishing not for the first time that he could fill in his own forms. "You can't wear them going through customs. Or the hat. Get rid of them."

"Not while there's this many punters marauding around." He continued to search through his satchel. I hurried to complete arrival forms. A crowd gathered.

"We're in deep shit," Jules hissed at me. "You should have given those to me, I'd have filled them in on the plane."

I couldn't believe what I was hearing. "Since when did you fill in your own arrival card?"

"Since I no longer need to behave like a spoilt brat to have you fuss over me." He lifted the brow of his cap and winked at me. "All I have to do now to get your attention is take my jeans off."

I couldn't help smiling. "Keep it down, we're attracting a crowd."

The throng had doubled in size. Even from a distance, I could hear the distinctive sound of cellphone photography happening.

"You're Julian, right?" A brave soul entered our sacred space.

I abandoned my form filling to see an ashen Julian still trying to locate his sunglasses.

"This'll teach me for not doing my share," he sighed, then turned to deal with his small band of followers. I recognized a few of the young girls - obsessive and compulsive stalkers who spent large sums each summer following the tour. Now, like hyenas feeding from a fallen carcass, they took the chance to get up close and personal with a jet-lagged Jules.

"That's right. How was the flight for you girls?"

"Great. How was first class?"

"So-so." Jules had on his best meet-the-fans voice though I knew he'd be hating every minute of this. "Shouldn't you girls be getting down through customs, picking up your stuff and all that?"

"Can we have a photo?"

"You going to be much longer, Mags?" Jules had a *save-me-I-promise-I'll-do-better* look on his face. His graciousness under pressure was a new experience.

I finished my Agriculture Declaration and started on Julian's. "Halfway there. You've got a couple of minutes."

"Not a problem, girls."

I heard a collective squeal of delight and tried to concentrate on putting the correct passport number in the correct place on the correct arrival card.

"Hey, hey, there's no need to push. Let's form a nice line here and everyone can get a picture."

I could see airport security approaching. We were causing a scene. I tried to complete the second form as fast as I could but the squealing and jostling in the line that had formed distracted me.

"What's the problem here?" The blue bulk of airport security in all its glory towered over me. Otis flanked Jules while Verne hovered around the ever-growing group.

Otis stepped forward, taking control. "No problem here, sir. Just a matter of Mr MacAvoy's fans taking a moment with him after the trip."

I could see the rest of the crew queuing ahead of us. They'd spilled past us from economy, where most of them travelled. I would never hear the end of this. I thanked the heavens this was the last gig and then I could have some quiet time with Jules.

"Pen, please." Under normal circumstances Jules would have spat the words in my ear. I decided I could get used to this new, improved man in my life. I knew he wanted the thick, autograph-signing marker and dug it out of my bag.

Things were going well now that the customs officials were organizing the autographs.

"Thanks so much, sir, for your help." Otis' authoritative tone boomed about the airport's warehouse-like space.

He turned to me. "Airport security is going to escort us through. They're worried about a mob forming, so they want us out of here ASAP."

This was the best news I'd heard in a while. "Great. Let's get moving then." I gathered my now completed arrival cards and declarations.

"Sorry, girls, no more time." Jules bid the disappointed mob farewell and we followed airport security around to the front of the penned passengers.

Amid the sounds of booing, shouts for Jules and assorted cellphone camera shutters going off, Jules removed his cap and we were processed by border security.

The crew would collect our luggage, so now it was just the usual mad dash for our arranged transportation and we were on our way again, to the next sterile hotel suite.

"It's not like you. In fact, you haven't been yourself for quite a while now." Jules wouldn't let my slip-up at the airport go. "What can I do to help?"

Only three pieces of his pre-show chocolate spiral remained and the heat from his half-drunk coffee had melted two squares into the white linen tablecloth. I despaired. I'd pretty much given up trying to keep anything of his clean, but today even the surrounding paraphernalia had consumed more food than me.

"Just stop going on about it and pour me another cup of coffee." If I didn't keep my caffeine levels up my head would explode.

"It's run out." He passed me his mug. "Here, have mine - I don't want any more."

Despite myself, I licked the sweet, molten chocolate from the base of the mug and took a drink. "God, it tastes like there's half a cow in here."

"Do you good." He grinned. "Full-fat milk. It'll refurbish your love-handles, give me something to grab."

I couldn't help checking out my backside. Despite my limited food intake it never seemed to get any smaller. Before I could craft a smart retort there was a sharp knock on the door.

Sheree entered. The look on her face turned my insides to ice, despite the warming coffee.

"You don't need to knock, darling." Jules was always pleased to see her, and oblivious to her seeming distress.

"What's wrong? Sit down." My concerns around Sheree were on constant alert, especially since the gross misconduct of her husband in Fiji.

"I just feel so sad this is our last night together," she said.

"They'll be other tours," Jules tried to console her.

She shook her head. "No, there won't - not for me. Jeremy won't allow it."

"He's not the boss of you." My nagging fear had become a reality – at least Jeremy hadn't tried to pull her before the end of the tour.

"Yeah, that's right." Jules agreed with me. "I am."

She smiled at that.

"He wants me to give this all up and have babies."

"What do you want?" I stroked her fine hair. "It's what you want that's important. Not what he wants."

"Yeah. You don't see me trying to tell Mags what to do." Jules looked pleased with himself.

I scowled at him. I hated him talking about us as a couple in front of Sheree – even though the entire crew now accepted our new status.

"You guys are the problem." Sheree wiped a single tear away from the side of her face. She walked away from me and settled herself on the couch. "Jeremy keeps holding you two up as the entire reason that the fabric of society is dissolving."

Jules looked hurt. "Why?"

"Because Mags is married."

"Oh, good grief. That." Jules sounded dismissive; as if Sheree were talking about a piece of old furniture I'd not gotten rid of yet. "Everyone knows that wasn't a real marriage - they barely spent any time together. Tell her, Mags."

I thought about it. I could barely remember the last time we'd shared a bed. I'd been sleeping on my own for years.

"That's what Jeremy's concerned about. He thinks I'm going to run off with you when you get sick of Mags."

"That's the most ridiculous thing I've ever heard." Jules came over to me, wrapping both arms protectively around my waist. He looked across to where Sheree sat on the small white couch, complete with its coffee stains and chocolate smears. "This woman is the most important thing in my life."

"Sorry, Shez." I felt the need to soften the edge of his words. I saw Jules realize what he'd said and felt sorry for him - no matter how he phrased it he risked pissing one of us off.

"Don't get me wrong, it's not like you're not gorgeous." He squeezed me tighter. I could feel the discomfort pouring forth from him.

Sheree laughed. "You two! I know, I know." She held her hands up, palms toward us, trying to stop the barrage of words. "You guys have something special, everyone sees that. Jeremy can be such an idiot. He doesn't understand that we're all family while we're away."

Her face took on a pinched look. "I guess he's worried Nick didn't understand that either, and now..."

There wasn't any need for her to finish the sentence; we all had a grasp of where she was going.

I extracted myself from Jules' loving but vice-like grip and sat down on the couch beside Sheree. "Look, Shez, here's how it is. I didn't mean to fall in love with Jules, and Nick and I had an *arrangement* for years." Everything in my life seemed backwards. I spent more time with Jules, I could be myself with Jules, I love being with Jules... My emotions were in a jumble. "The time I spent with Nick was like being at work. It- it's hard to explain."

"No, it's not." She looked at me, her clear blue eyes almost seeing through me; she was here, but somewhere else at the same time. "When you're with Jules you're alive. I understand that. I haven't seen you with Nick much, but when I have you've been like a dead person. Almost two-dimensional. Whenever you're with Jules you're animated and effective. Life kind of explodes out of you in a rainbow of color."

I'd never heard it explained like that before.

"We've always been able to see what great friends you are, and now that you've both worked out how much you love each other, well..." Sheree left the sentence unfinished. Much like my marriage.

"So the important thing is do you feel like that when you're with Jeremy?" I asked.

"I do. Yes." She nodded. "But I can't stand the thought of having to give up you guys."

I gave her a hug. "You don't have to give us up."

"But then I might lose him."

"If he's dumb enough to dump you because you won't give us up he doesn't deserve you." I could barely keep my contempt for Jeremy out of my voice.

Sheree opened her mouth to say something, then thought better of it and closed her lips.

Jules took over from me. "Look, marriage is a base-camp relationship."

"You've never been married." Then Shez looked at me. "And your marriage is nothing more than a financial arrangement, it appears."

"That doesn't matter." Jules took her hands in his, forcing her to look him straight in the eyes. "What I know is," he frowned, "And I'll qualify that by saying that the most important relationship I've ever had has been with Mags."

He caught my eye and a strange sense of serenity flowed through me, matched by the look of love and trust on his face.

"When things are right with Mags, at my base-camp, then it doesn't matter what's going on anywhere else. It doesn't matter what crap the press are writing about me, or how badly the shows are going, or how much I hate the director on the last video shoot, or what an asshole the producer is in the studio."

He took a breath and squeezed her fingers a little tighter. I could see the small blue veins through the translucent white skin on the back of her hands - spent blood making its way back to her heart for vital nourishment. If Sheree gave up dancing, I wondered how Jeremy would nourish the soul of the woman he loved, for she'd surely wither without us.

Jules continued on. "All that matters is I have a safe haven to bring all of that experience back to. And someone who supports and loves me and will let me untangle all that bitterness and vileness. Mags allows me to unload on her."

I piped in. "And Jules allows me to unload on him."

"I'm learning." He replied.

It was true. I'd mothered him for years and I still struggled to let anyone look after me.

Jules continued on. "So you see, we have this equal partnership. This safe place, where we can venture out into the vile blue yonder, get our asses kicked, and then limp back to be patched up before we head on out again."

"I'd never thought about it like that." Sheree wriggled her hands free from Jules, clasping them protectively around herself.

"Most people don't and that's why their relationships don't work. It took Mags to make me see all of this."

"It did?" I found that statement hard to believe.

Now he took my hand, placing my palm against his smooth, freshly shaved cheek. "Yes, it did, and I will be forever grateful to you for showing me this wonderful way of living."

"But you my darling girl," Jules continued to hold my hand while he spoke to Sheree, "Will have to work out what you want from your life."

"I don't want to let you down, Julian." Sheree stared at her clasped hands while she spoke, pain running like a thread through her voice. "Or you, Mags. You've both been really good to me."

"It's our last night," I offered, "You're not letting us down."

"But the next tour?"

"Who knows if there'll ever be another tour?" Jules didn't sound at all concerned. "You just go out there tonight and give it heaps."

"You guys are great." Sheree embraced us both.

Why did I feel as if I'd just witnessed the end of an era?

CHAPTER SIXTEEN

Many a time I'd watched Jules from the sidelines, most often at the start of a show, but there's always something special about the final show in a tour.

The crowd knew Jules' relationship with his record company had come to an end. So it seemed even more pertinent to be watching what I knew to be the final song, the song preceding the final curtain call.

Jules had attempted to leave the stage twice already, but the fans, all eighty thousand of them, nearly brought the arena down with their stamping demands that he return to the stage.

Now, in the final chorus of the last song of the tour, I experienced a new feeling - a premonition that I'd never see Jules like this again, giving himself to his adoring fans.

A chill ran down my spine despite the heat backstage.

He'd been crucified by the record company, yet the fans still loved him - they were here in their adoring thousands.

I caught my breath.

The feeling passed.

The last bars of the final song hung in the air.

Jules stood stock still. A single blue spotlight held his perfect image against the blacked out stage.

The light went out.

The crowd erupted again.

The wall of sound washed over me, just as the backstage crew hustled me to the front of the stage.

In a second we were blinded by the harsh white light thrown over us from the high rigging.

Jules held my right hand, Sheree my left, beyond them stood Dan and Ted and Fred. The entire crew lined the edge of the stage. Jules bowed to his adoring crowd. We all followed his lead, a ripple of domino people falling from his center.

The roar of the crowd obliterated every thought or sound from the stage.

We bowed again.

Screams and the thumping of feet overwhelmed me. Adrenaline ran through my veins as we bowed for the third and final time.

Each of us peeled off stage. Jules the last to leave. The crowd continued to yell and scream and thump.

I knew the moment the stadium lights came up because the screaming and thumping began to ease. They would all begin to move away, as we were.

The limo would be waiting at the back of the stadium for us.

I handed Jules a towel.

Pinpricks of sweat bubbled from his face. His shirt stuck to his back, he looked as if he had been standing in a sauna.

He was unusually quiet.

I didn't want to break the spell, the silence - be the first to speak.

Without saying a word, we entered the limo.

Otis and Verne, our ever-present shadows, clambered in after us.

I knew it was over – the endless, fevered chase for that tiny star.

I think he did too.

Jules had promised me time - time without touring, time without the bodyguards, time just for us.

Time to work it out, he said.

Touring was over, but the bodyguards and the band weren't prepared to leave us alone just yet.

They'd demanded the end-of-tour debrief and party. This limo ride would be the nearest I would get, for the moment, to time alone.

Many roundabouts later and in the dark we arrived at the Reef House Hotel. The understated but elegant restaurant was filled with well-dressed and well-behaved Australians. Brent, the front-of-house manager, greeted us, the broad twang of his elongated Australian syllables immediately putting me at ease.

"Welcome to the Reef House. How was your trip?"

"Great, thank you."

Julian stood silently beside me. Another select mob had assaulted us as we arrived. News had traveled fast of our destination.

"I'll arrange for your luggage to go to your room."

"Mags, you take Jules and I'll sort out the paperwork and luggage." Dan knew we wanted to be alone. I was grateful he came to my aid.

"You're in Suite 402," Brent told us. "Come with me

and we'll take a short tour on the way."

Brent was obviously gay. As we walked around the exclusive hotel it was apparent to me that he was sizing up Julian.

"And this is the number one spa in Australia." We stood between a glorious seawater pool, which glowed iridescent aqua-green in the evening light, and a petite, gated enclosure that reminded me of a Mexican homestead. "Be sure to book a massage and treatment while you're here. The girls are wonderful."

We followed Brent through lush vegetation, over cobbled pathways and up a small flight of wooden stairs onto a beautiful terrace with a swinging wicker couch.

The room with its terracotta tiled floor, white louver doors and wickerwork furniture spoke to me of all things romantic and long, hot Indian summers.

Jules immediately made his way to the master suite and threw himself across the extra-large king-size bed. The half-draped mosquito net swung lazily in the breeze from the overhead fan.

"Comfy." He looked across at me and Brent. "A man could have some real fun here."

I realized immediately from the look on Brent's face he'd have happily joined Jules.

"Thanks so much for the tour. I can take it from here." I wasn't just talking about settling us into the room.

Brent looked taken aback. A flash of understanding passed between us and his face flushed. "Enjoy your stay and remember that reception is available twenty-four hours a day."

Not the only thing available twenty-four hours a day, I thought.

"Thank you so much." I ushered him out of the suite.

I made my way back quickly to our room. "Julian, you're an arsehole!"

"What?"

"Don't play the innocent with me. Flirting with that poor man."

"Jealous?"

"No," I lied. The thought of that man anywhere near Jules set up an irrational feeling of protectiveness. "We should unpack."

Jules leapt from the bed and swept me into his arms. "Let's not." His husky voice, the tousled look of him and the pleading look in his eyes dissolved my intent.

I coughed. "Jules. Really."

It seemed like weeks since we'd been intimate. The screaming tour schedule, the pressure of press and fans, plus general exhaustion had somehow kept us apart.

He took my hand. It trembled in his. "Come sit with me for a while." With sureness of foot he led me back to that great stretch of bed.

I'd spent hours sitting with him on beds in strange hotel suites. Why should this be any different?

"You're trembling." He'd noticed.

Flicking my hair back over my ear, his fingers lingered on the side of my neck. He must be able to feel the beating of my heart – it was all I could hear.

I took his hand between both of mine. Held it tight. Tried to regain some control, some kind of composure. Tried to not feel like a stumbling, virginal schoolgirl.

"You're cold?" It was an insane question.

I shook my head. "No." My body continued to betray me. I wanted him.

"Come here." He extracted his hand from mine and expertly laced both arms around me in one swift movement. It was like being encased by a boa constrictor. He placed me back on the bed, still holding me tight. I shuddered with delight.

Cocking his head to one side, he reminded me of an inquisitive puppy. "You're not cold, are you, Mags?"

I shook my head again.

"You love me, don't you?"

"Yes." The word erupted from my throat in a single quivering breath.

Jules said, "I've loved you for a long time." He leaned down, pressing himself against the length of my upper body, and kissed me.

A Long, slow kiss, full of conviction and promise.

I lost myself in him. In the glorious moment of connection. My blood pulsed through me. My head spun. My hands reached for him.

Grasping. Clawing. Clutching.

I ran my fingers through his hair, down his neck, across his broad back.

His tongue found mine. Snaked its way into the recess of my mouth. I imagined other parts of him snaking their way into my depths.

Heat ran through me. My body quaked at his touch. He pressed harder, deeper, with more urgency.

I met his passion. Weeks of pent-up longing flooded through me. I scratched at his shirt. It came away over his head, the material barely slipping between our mouths before his was back on mine.

He lay naked on the bed. The fully glory of him,

unadorned, before me. My mind flashed back to the stolen moments when I'd watched him working out before the mirror. And here he lay now, waiting for me.

"Mags."

His voice, the voice I knew from thousands of tracks, the voice I'd listened to for years, sounded different. Burning. Husky.

I knelt above him and my knees went weak with anticipation. The bed almost undulated under me.

Jules leaned up onto his elbows. The expansive slope of his hairy chest met at the savannah of his stomach. Beyond that was his densely covered pubic area, where his erect penis lay like a fallen log of the forest.

I loved him and I wanted him and nothing would stand in my way. I tore at my clothes, buttons popping and pinging their way around the room. I didn't care. All I wanted was Jules.

His eyes never left me as I unwrapped myself exposing my body to him. Longing for the touch of his flesh and knowing I'd soon feel the naked heat of him against me.

"I've missed you." His words dissolved into my hair. At the strong and sure touch of his hands on my buttock cheeks a surge of lust shot to the pit of my belly.

The connection to him, the universe and anything beyond seemed complete. The circuit of emotion and love running between us gaining momentum and building power.

My body came to life at his touch; he played me like the musicians in the band played their instruments. As his mouth and fingers danced across my naked flesh, as I surrendered to the beauty of him, I felt more complete and whole than I had in my entire life.

"I love you, Jules." As the words fell from my mouth, his made its way to the center of me.

I felt his tongue lapping at me and lost myself in the overwhelming pleasure.

I've no idea how long he ministered to me, but the rolling sensation of orgasm came in like the sea creeping across the bay below us. Little waves to begin with, but before long I was swimming in the sensation of him.

I shivered as he entered me.

Strong.

Forceful.

Concentrated.

"You're beautiful." The only words I needed to hear from him.

He stroked himself in and out, bringing me to the brink of orgasm again, and then expertly allowing the peak to recede before bringing me back to the edge.

Jules looked down into my eyes, dropped his mouth over mine and breathed into me as he thrust himself hard and fast inside.

I fell over the edge again, but this time I took him with me, the shuddering of his body reflecting the spasm of mine. He whimpered softly against the nape of my neck, the weight of his body slumping on top of my sweating torso.

"God, I love you."

My inclination to disbelieve a man who says he loves you as soon as you've finished making love evaporated. I knew Jules and I knew we loved each other. I knew he was the one I'd been waiting for.

A sense of wonder stole over me. I dozed in the comfort and safety of my lover's arms as the chaos of our separate lives continued to rage around us.

The gruesome tour wrap-up party behind us, Jules insisted on spoiling me. I detested the idea of a massage, but he wasn't giving up easily.

"We're at the best spa in the country and I really think you'll enjoy this."

"I can't think of anything more repulsive than having a perfect stranger's hands on me."

"Trust me."   He touched my arm and I had an immediate physical memory of our lovemaking; electrical impulses from him ran through my body.

"Why would I want anyone else massaging me when I've got you?"   I returned his loving touch, my hands enjoying the warmth and span of his body.

"You'll enjoy it. I promise you."

I entered the scented and serene surrounds of the spa. Immediately the intense, sweet air assaulted me and the anxiety I'd been carrying began to slip away.

With great tenderness, Jules held my hand. Aware we were on public view – albeit in the confines of the discreet spa - my instinct was still to pull away.

Jules gripped my hand tighter. "You don't have to worry, Mags. You know they design these places for people like us, don't you?"

"I don't want to be people like us," I hissed. I had a fleeting thought of Nick but banished it to the far recesses of my mind.

Jules saw the clouds behind my eyes. "I meant celebrities, not married lovers."

"Don't say it."   The words, the truth, fell like heavy

cables across my heart. "I don't want to be either of those things."

Jules shrugged. "You've changed your circumstances, there's not much chance of me suddenly losing my celebrity status." He squeezed my hand again, and despite my misgivings I warmed to his touch. "Short of vanishing off the face of the earth, but I don't think Richard Branson has built a city on the moon yet."

"I'm sure it won't be long." Jules had been harping on for ages about flying into space. "Besides, it's enough trouble just flying you first class around the earth."

He laughed and I felt my sense of ease return.

"Good morning, how are you both?" A petite woman dressed in a black oriental-looking top and black pants greeted us. I noticed the edges of the shirt were trimmed with a fine gold band and her hair, twisted into a topknot, held a fragrant frangipani flower pleated between the layers. "Please follow me."

We were led further into the perfumed interior of the building and instructed to seat ourselves on a comfortable couch. A pitcher of water and two glasses sat on a copper tray, together with two small forms.

"Please make yourselves comfortable, have something to drink, and complete the short medical questionnaires. I'll be back with you shortly."

Frangipani girl poured us each a glass of water from the jug. In the humid heat, condensation ran in rivulets down the side of the clear vessel. The clinking of ice on the crystal glasses and the sight of little chunks of lime and lemon evoked feelings of subtropical delight.

Jules looked at me hopefully.

"Fill in your own form, pal. I'm on strike." I was

enjoying my new status as his partner, not his employee.

Jules laughed, the sound filling the compact room.

Frangipani girl returned about five minutes later with a look-alike and went through our completed forms.

"These all look to be in order. We will be looking after you today. Please come through."

We followed them up a set of dark brown stairs, which led to a long, narrow hallway with many doors running off it.

"It looks like a brothel," Julian whispered into my ear.

I thumped him swiftly in the arm. "Behave."

The frangipani twins led us to a bathroom with gleaming tiled surfaces. Tropical flowers floated in small wooden bowls and an oil burner simmered quietly in the corner, filling the enclosed space with a relaxing scent.

"Please undress, place your clothes in the locker and take a shower - there are plenty of towels. You will find a robe for each of you and sandals for your feet."

A vast sea of rolled-up towels were stacked neatly in baskets on the other side of the room. A tidal wave of toweling. "Then take a seat in the waiting area when you are ready."

The frangipani twins closed the door behind them as they left the room.

"More and more like a brothel. Are you sure these girls won't ask us if we want a happy ending?" Jules smirked at me.

"You're not making this any easier for me." I relieved my feet of shoes. "I'll give you a happy ending. Now get your gear off."

"Here, let me help you gets yours off." He was by my side in a moment, fingers dancing over the flesh at the base of my throat, expertly attending to the unbuttoning of my thin muslin shift. His lips followed where his fingers had been, working his way at speed down my bodice.

Giggling, I grasped his head in my hands, stopping his descent. "Get off! We're supposed to be preparing for a massage."

"I like our kind of massage. Me massaging you with my entire body."

I kissed him on the forehead. "I like that too, but they'll be waiting for us. Now let me go, and get undressed."

"Only trying to help."

"Well, your kind of help means it'd be another hour before we even reached the waiting room and I'd need a second another shower to boot."

Jules stripped swiftly and stepped into the shower. I was tempted to take him up on his offer of help. My body, still warm from his caresses this morning, responded to the sight of his sodden nakedness with a maddening and insatiable desire to touch him.

I tore my eyes away from the feast that was his beautiful bulk and concentrated on getting myself into the adjoining shower before I lost my sense of control. Again.

Robed and sandaled and trying hard not to look at each other – and failing - we waited for the return of the frangipani twins.

They arrived in silence. I had the overwhelming feeling of being in some modern-day convent with these young novices about to attend to my every need.

"Please come through." They led us to a dimly lit room dominated by the color orange. Center-stage sat two massage beds. We were directed to two chairs on one side of the room and opposite a deep, dual spa bath. The frangipani twins sat on the floor in front of us and guided our feet into large copper bowls of warm water. Heat oozed up my body. The twins dropped scented essential oils into the water and we physically relaxed.

Hands gently massaged my feet and I closed my eyes, lost in the intoxicating feelings running through my body.

Julian sighed.

Too soon the massaging ceased. I opened my eyes and the fragrant twins were drying their hands.

"When we begin your massage we will burn some smudge." A small bowl of dried leaves was passed to each of us for us to sniff. "This is a traditional Aboriginal smudge made from the leaves of the rainforest. It's a ritual that clears dark energies and creates a safe and sacred space for us to work within."

We were then passed three bottles of oil.

"We use three blends of oil here. Please choose the one you would like."

The first smelt sharp; I could taste citrus at the back of my throat. The second had overtones of rose and the third reminded me of a damp forest.

I chose the third oil.

"I'll have this one as well." Jules seemed reluctant to give back the bottle.

"This is a subtle blend of wood scents, designed to clear the mind and refresh the spirit. It's like walking in the forest after rain."

Our feet were dried and we were directed to the two massage tables.

"We are going to leave the room. Please take off your robes, lie on the tables on your front and drape these towels across yourselves. We will be back shortly."

Already feeling somewhat in a relaxed state, I did as I was told without any fear. Awareness flooded my naked body. The soft towel beneath and the snug feel of the larger towel draped above cocooned me. My face slipped into the open space at the top of the table, supported on each side by small, soft towels. I floated in midair.

Jules let out another contented sigh. "Didn't I tell you this would be wonderful?"

He had and now I understood. "I can't believe I haven't done this before."

The frangipani twins returned. My towel was rearranged and strong hands stroked my body through the material. I became aware of relaxing music playing in the background. How could I have missed that until now?

As the sweet fragrance of burning leaves and herbs filled the room, my towel was draped down, exposing my back to the subtropical, scented air. Warm hands covered in smooth oil began working the length of my back in long, swirling strokes. A small sigh escaped my lips and I sank deeper into the table, my muscles surrendering to the sensual pummeling.

I began to drift. The whirling thoughts in my brain slowed. My awareness of things outside of the confines of my own body began to diminish. As my frangipani twin worked my body, no muscle group left untouched, my senses literally left me.

I became one large and lifeless jellyfish.

Somewhere in the hour and a half I lay there, being pounded by a she-devil, I turned over and barely noticed I was no longer lying on my stomach.

The hairband was removed from my ponytail and my scalp was expertly massaged. I had little awareness of the table I lay on, or my body. I was at one with some divine spiritual being, some larger-than-life cosmic presence that had me in its incorporeal grip.

Too soon, the magic hands fell away from me and we were advised that our frangipani angels would wait for us outside.

"I can't move." Julian's voice drifted across the small space that separated us, weaseling its way into my floating consciousness.

"I don't want to move." My limbs felt like dead weights. The effort required to bring myself back into my body and direct any worthwhile activity from my recalcitrant appendages seemed insurmountable.

"Get up," Jules urged.

"Do I have to?"

"Yes. They're waiting for us. Now come on."

I moaned.

The soft orange world we'd resided in for the last hour or so swam before my eyes, as I struggled to sit up.

My hairband lay to my right and my robe to my left. I dropped to the floor, feeling like a cosmonaut just returning from orbit, and fought my way back into the robe.

I turned in time to catch Jules slipping his over the splendor of his nakedness. A bolt of wholesome lust brought me hurtling back to the present moment.

His beauty astounded me and I still found it hard to believe he wanted me.

We were greeted again by one of the frangipani twins and directed to another airy, whitewashed room. Dark-stained shutters were propped open over the window alcoves, allowing the tropical morning breeze to enter the space.

"Please take your time and drink some tea. It is full of herbs to help flush your body of toxins."

Our frangipani twin poured us each a cup of fragrant green tea from the earthenware pot, another delightful aroma mingling with the heavily scented air.

It seemed as if I'd passed back in time and arrived at a jungle bathhouse. I took a sip of the warming tea, completely at peace with myself, with Julian and with the world.

Jules looked across at me. "I want it to be like this always."

He put his teacup down and dropped to his knees on the floor before me. "Marry me. Stay with me forever. I love you so much and I can't stand the thought of ever being away from you."

His declaration took me by surprise.

"I want it to be like this always too, but I have to sort my life out."

"You can do that easily. We'll get a good attorney."

He looked so hopeful. So adorable. I loved him so much.

He offered, "I'll give up touring."

"But you love touring."

He shook his head. "Nah, not so much - not after this last one. I want off this mad merry-go-round. We'll settle down somewhere nice, somewhere like this."

"I'd like that." Then I thought about everyone on tour. "What about Shez and Ted and Dan and the band?"

A flash of concern crossed his features. We were a family; we'd been together a long time. "They'll be fine. They're at the top of their game as well. Every one of them will have more work opportunities than they'll know what to do with."

He picked up my hands, kissing each of my open palms in turn. "We can do it, I know we can. We can leave all the shit behind us and make a life for ourselves together."

He'd convinced me. "Yes. Yes, I'll do it. I'll sort it all out and I will marry you."

Jules picked me up in his arms, in that sweet-scented tropical bathhouse, and hugged me. "I promise you - we'll be happy. We will have a great life."

I believed him.

I'd always believed in him.

That's why I'd followed him all over the world.

CHAPTER SEVENTEEN

"They're a pain." I couldn't hide my disgust.

Home and hiding out at Jules' estate, we were on video-link to Dan. The record company had come crawling back. Apparently, while Jules was on tour he'd written some of the most amazing material they'd heard from him.

"Just shows what a little bit of misery can do for the boy's writing talent." Dan's enthusiasm boomed through the link.

I didn't want to hear this.

"So they're arranging a small, exclusive gig. Corporate ranks, press, the usual marketing crowd."

"I'm not doing it." Jules sat sulkily in the corner of the room. "They dumped me, they can fuck off."

"You're still on contract, mate - they never officially canceled. They've been on the blower saying it was all a publicity stunt to increase sales for the tour."

"Blah-de-fucking-blah." Jules had a look of thunder on his face.

My stomach knotted. We were never going to get off

the road and lead a quiet life – I could see that now. If I wanted to be with Jules then this was how it would be - tears, tantrums, and a plethora of other people who had a stake in our lives.

I tried to soothe the savage beast beside me. "It might not be so bad."

He turned on me. "How the fuck can it not be so bad?" Despair and rage had taken to his face like a sculptor takes to a piece of marble. His beautiful, even features were gone.

My breath caught in my throat. For a second I barely recognized him as the man I loved. Overtaken by a coughing fit, I couldn't answer him. I merely shook my head, at a loss to see a way out of this latest predicament.

"God, are you okay?" Jules patted my back. "Can I get you a glass of water?"

I nodded. The coughing fit continuing.

"What the hell's going on there? Julian, you can't just walk away." Dan had been abandoned. Through one teary eye, I could see him getting redder in the face as he tried to deal with his troublesome charge.

"Nothing's going on," I spluttered between another set of coughs.

"The thought of me going back to that crappy record company is killing her as well." Jules' face had softened, edged with concern. He passed me a glass of water and resumed his patting, rubbing mini circles with his hand in the middle of my shoulder-blades.

I took a sip of the cool liquid and suppressed another urge to cough. He hooked a stray strand of hair behind my ear that had escaped the prison of my ponytail. The loving gesture was the antithesis of the way he'd been behaving a few moments ago. I realized that was what I loved so much about him - I never knew what would happen from one moment to the next. Life had become an exhilarating rollercoaster ride and I wanted to share the leading seat next to him.

"Fuck them all." Jules was speaking directly to Dan again.

"You know you're going to have to do it." Dan's usual fatherly tone sounded comical when overlaid by a slight chipmunk voice effect from the laptop's microphone.

"They can sue me."

I cut in. "They *would* sue you."

"Well, then we could have a quiet life."

Dan cut across our conversation. "You can lead a quiet life when your contract expires."

"Another two years of hell." Jules continued to look miserable.

I tapped his clenched fist and he opened his hand at my touch. His palm carried a sheen of moisture. "It will go quickly," I reassured him.

"Life does - that's what I'm scared of." He looked into my eyes and it seemed almost as if he could see right inside of me. "I don't want any more of it running by without you being the focus of it."

I patted his clammy hand. "I can wait for you on the sidelines. It's what I've been doing for a long time."

"But I don't want you on the sidelines anymore. I want the world to know that we're together and that I love you."

Before I could answer, Dan interrupted us. "Mags is on the right-"

Jules dropped the lid of the laptop and then kissed me.

"That dealt to him." Jules whispered the words

between our closely touching lips.

"He won't be happy," I whispered back.

"Fuck him."

"How about fuck me?" I couldn't resist repeating him.

"Sounds like a plan." He took me in his arms and carried me through to the bedroom.

"He's not going to leave you alone."

"I'm not going to leave you alone."

"You're going to have to do it, you know."

Jules had laid me on the bed and was now concentrating on removing my clothes. "I know, but they can sweat about it for a while."

"So you won't hate going on tour?" My panties were being wriggled off my bottom and down my legs.

"I will." He looked up while kissing me on the inner thigh. "But you'll be there, so it won't be too bad."

His tongue lingered where his kiss had just been.

"You're teasing me."

"I know. You like that."

I let go of the thoughts about touring and concentrated on the small sparks of pleasure igniting under the caress of Jules' lips.

Packed with every industry record executive, marketing person, magazine publisher and promoter that the recording company could get through the door, there hadn't been a launch like it in years. The room buzzed with anticipation, as various television networks jockeyed with each other for the best vantage point.

Jules sounded morose. "Oh, God. It looks like I'm back."

"You never went anywhere," I whispered to him.

"And being welcomed with open arms." Dan's enthusiasm wasn't catching.

"Where's the bar?" Frederick and Ted were always up for a party and didn't seem to care that Jules would rather have been at home in bed.

"Julian." Steve Zimmerman, the CEO of Zmak records, arrived at our sides when we'd barely entered the expansive room. He pumped Jules' hand as if he were meeting a long-lost friend, which I suppose in a way he could have been. "How are you doing after the tour?"

Dan glared at Jules from over the aging executive's shoulder. Steve not only failed in the style stakes, he looked as if he'd spent far too many nights on the town with out-of-control groupies.

"Behave," I hissed at Jules. For some reason I couldn't fathom, I desperately wanted the night to go well.

"It's great to be having a break." At least he had the appearance of having left the vitriol at the door.

"You wrote some amazing material while you were on the road," Steve gushed. Now I wanted to escape.

The crew collected like a small bunch of shiny marbles over by the circular bar. Zmak had hired a new hip club on the southern side of town, the Portabello, to hold the launch – or re-launch as it was being billed.

Beautiful people filled the room and I felt dowdy and out of place. Jules always insisted he was out of place too. We were the perfect couple, it seemed to me.

I made my way to our marble allies. Everyone wanted a piece of Jules, so progress was slow. We had to stop every couple of steps for another important and unknown person to congratulate him on his success. Jules charmed each and every one of them. The entire room seemed spellbound by his natural charisma.

"I am so over this," Jules muttered as he nuzzled the nape of my neck. "It's times like these I think drinking would be a great idea."

I couldn't hear the camera shutters clicking over the din around us, but I saw the flash of accompanying light as photographers took their chance to get pictures of us together. I resigned myself to our every intimate moment being documented by the press and distorted by hack tabloid journalists.

"I so get that." I passed Jules his sparkling mineral water and chugged back half of the energy drink Sheree passed me.

Jeremy stood behind her, hiding in the shadows where he belonged. I hadn't gotten over his performance at the docks when we'd last seen him. As far as I was concerned if we never saw him again it would be too soon.

Jules must have read my mind. "What's that piece of shit doing here?"

"Ssh. Shez will hear you."

"I don't care if she does. He's no longer welcome anywhere near me."

I knew Jules wanted something to get pissed off about so he could walk out.

"Come on." I took his arm and moved him away from the rest of the band. "Let's go and find Dan and see what the program for the night is."

"Yeah. The sooner we get this over and done with, the sooner we can get out of here."

"You're charming their socks off as usual." Dan slapped Jules on the back.

"Well, I won't be charming anyone's socks off if you

don't get that asshole out of here." Jules pointed his chin in the direction of Jeremy, who continued to lurk in the shadow of his wife. I couldn't help thinking the image reflected their life together.

"Just let them alone." Dan beat me to the admonishment. "It's time to get you out the front again."

Then I saw them. Just as Jules picked up the microphone and the band launched into his intro.

Nick, with three other men, standing to the side of the room. His face masklike, showing little or no emotion.

I didn't recognize two of the men who stood with him, but I knew the third. I would never forget his face.

Young Elvis.

What the hell were they doing here and how had Nick gotten past the door without me being alerted to his presence?

The edges of the room began to close in on me. My throat tightened.

Jules hit his stride in the opening moments of the new song. The crowd went wild.

Nick caught my eye, then looked away.

I knew I should move toward them. Find out why they were here, but my body refused to acknowledge every order my brain made.

I couldn't face another scene with Nick. Not now. Not tonight.

Where was Otis? I needed to have them all discreetly removed.

"Nick's here," I managed to stammer the words into Dan's ear.

"Where?" The urgency in his voice told me all I needed to know.

"Over there."   I pointed in the direction of the threesome.

In the millisecond it had taken me to get Dan's attention they had gone. I began to sway.

"It's okay, I've got you."   Dan had a firm grip on my elbow. "Otis needs to get rid of them."   He maneuvered me through the crowd.

I heard Jules miss a lyric line. I looked up, tried to convey to him it was all right. I caught a worried frown as he stuttered a recovery.

Dan deposited me in the nearest seat.   There were plenty - the excited crowd had moved forward to the front of the stage.

Suddenly there was a blinding light, a camera in my face, a microphone thrust under my chin.

"What do you have to say about the rumors circulating that you and Julian are having an affair?"

I tried to shield my eyes from the light. "What?"

"She's got no comment. Now fuck off!"   Dan tried to push the reporter away.

They jostled, but the camera remained on me.

"Steve here-" the reporter motioned to Young Elvis, who stood to one side with Nick "-says he was given the flick by Julian in favor of you.   Your husband over there seems to think that's correct.   What comment do you have to make about that?"

I could see Young Elvis and Nick, both stony-faced and glowering at me from the side of the white lights.

"I told you, mate, she's got no comment, so you can get out of here."

I could no longer hear Jules singing.   He arrived at my side.

"What are you doing?" I hissed at him. "You should be up on stage." He had a contract. He couldn't be here with me.

"I'm getting rid of these idiots."

"What? My ex-husband and your ex-lover?" It all seemed quite surreal. My grip on sanity was slipping.

"We're not idiots," Young Elvis spoke up. "I love you and you treat me like shit." There was a wild look in his eye.

The cameraman turned toward him and Nick. Then I noticed that the pool of light included Jeremy and it all started to make sense.

Nick spoke, his eyes never leaving me. "I thought you loved me, but you left me for this pervert." The last word stung. He might as well have just punched me.

Jules tensed at my side. I had to keep him away from these men. I told him, "Jules, you need to get back on stage. They want you to make a scene."

"Well, then, they're going to get one," he growled.

Where the hell was Otis? I looked at Dan.

"Now, come on lads, let's take this outside." Dan tried to calm things down.

Tension escalated. The band's playing had come to an unprofessional end.

"You can't sweep under the carpet the way this pervert has been behaving." Jeremy voiced his opinion, his confidence bolstered by the gathering crowd. "First he's screwing men and then he's screwing married women." Jeremy pushed Nick forward. "I mean, his wife works for the prick and now he's screwing her."

"Stop it." I'd heard enough. I knew the cameraman had enough to crucify Jules, but it was the look on Nick's face that concerned me more than anything.

I was in love with Jules, yet on some level I still felt responsible for Nick's wellbeing. For his happiness and for what others thought about him. The shackles of marriage were hard to shake.

"Come on, I need to get you out of here." Jules lifted me from the seat.

"You need to get back on stage."

"No, I'm not getting back up there."

"You've got a contract..." My protestations fell on ears that refused to hear.

"The only contract I want from now on is one in marriage with you."

He still wanted me to marry him. Even after all this.

Otis had been not more than a step behind Jules. He stepped between us and the camera. "Time you guys were out of here," he told the cameraman. The man with the microphone took one look at Otis and went white.

Verne turned up on cue. He and Otis were a formidable team, but I wondered how much the cameraman had managed to catch of the conversation between Jules and me.

Nick's eyes had never moved from me. He stood, flanked by Young Elvis and Jeremy. They reminded me of the three monkeys.

No hear.

No see.

No speak.

Only I had a feeling there'd be little chance of those three principles applying to these boys.

"You guys aren't authorized to cover this event, you need to remove yourselves from the premises." Dan rejoined the fray, directing his comments at the hostile reporters. I noticed the rest of the band had abandoned the stage and were also gathering on the edges of the circle.

Nick remained motionless. In all the time I'd known him he'd never looked so unwell.

My skin began to prickle and my stomach bubbled like a cauldron.

"Jules," I whispered in his ear, aware that the mike still hovered close and could be on. "We need to get out of here."

"It's okay. The lads have it under control."

The hairs on the back of my neck rose. The urge to vomit came over me. "It's nowhere near under control."

Otis and Verne tried to manhandle the two pressmen and the three monkeys out of the room.

The band began to jostle amongst themselves. The inner circle was now surrounded by an outer circle of guests that ran four or five deep.

Claustrophobia clawed at me like a cat.

Otis, ever on the alert, spotted Jeremy lining him up for a punch. Stepping back, Otis smoothly diverted the blow toward the cameraman, connecting Jeremy's fist with the cameraman's head. The force of the blow dislodged the camera on his shoulder, the sound as it crashed on the polished concrete floor cutting through the room.

"Fuckin' idiot." The interviewer dropped his mike and took a swing at Jeremy.

Jeremy ducked. The interviewer's fist connected with Young Elvis' jaw. Young Elvis seized the opportunity and took to the interviewer, behaving like a street-fighter.

The shockwave traveled from its epicenter out through

the wave of surrounding people, and all hell broke loose.

I lost sight of the core group of agitators as Jules, Otis and Verne surrounded me, a shield of man-flesh. Through the gaps between their bodies I saw what looked like an out-of-control barroom brawl. Chairs came down on hapless people, glasses and cans were flying across the room like liquid grenades, and I spotted bare skin as clothing was torn from bodies.

The sound of women screaming and men cursing accompanied me out of the room as the boys hustled me through the bar area and out into a back room of the nightclub.

"Fuck. Fuck. Fuck. Fuck." Jules banged the heel of his hand into his forehead as he spoke each expletive.

"Calm down," Otis told him. Like there was any chance of that.

"I won't fucking calm down." Jules stalked around the storeroom like a caged animal.

"Please, can you cut the language?" I was shaking so badly now he'd let go of me I thought I might fall over.

Jules again rushed to my side. "Shit. Sorry." His arms surrounded me and I fell into the familiar, safe warmth of his body.

I concentrated hard on breathing in slowly through my nose, holding the breath for three counts and then exhaling. I could do without a panic attack right now.

"It's getting uglier out there by the minute." Verne dashed back into the room, presumably having ducked out to check on the brawl's progress. "We need to get you two out of here before the cops arrive."

"What about the rest of the band?" Would I ever stop worrying about them all?

As if on cue Dan burst through the door, closely followed by Fred and Ted. Dan's shirt had a huge rip down the back and blood from a split lip dripped down the front of his chin.

A second later, Sheree rushed into the room with Jeremy at her heels.

"Fucking get him out of here," Jules exploded. "He caused this riot!"

Jules leapt toward Jeremy, who made the sensible decision to stand behind Sheree.

"You're responsible for all of this!" Jules' voice echoed off the aluminum beer kegs that lined the wall. "Stop hiding behind a woman - get out here."

"At least I'm not a faggot who screws married women!" Jeremy shot the remark over Sheree's shoulder.

"I'll fucking kill him!"

Otis threw an arm around Jules' waist as he lunged again for Jeremy. "Come on. We need you to stay cool and get your lady out of here." Otis spoke calmly, taking control of the situation.

"Where's Nick and why did you bring him here?" I cast my question across the backs of Jules and Otis.

"Why do you care?" Jeremy couldn't keep the contempt out of his voice. "You cast him aside for that pervert."

"Jeremy, stop it." Sheree attempted to maneuver him like an overgrown toddler, past us and to the door beyond.

"He won't stop it. Don't you see that?" Jules' voice was almost a whisper.

He broke free from Otis and came again to my side, collecting me in his trembling arms. "It's over. It's done."

He nuzzled his face into the side of my neck and whispered in my ear, "I'll never work again. Not now. Not after this."

CHAPTER EIGHTEEN

"You've got a nerve turning up here." Jeremy's voice was as cold as the marble floor I stood on.

"It's my house; I have every right to be here." I stalked past him. "Where is he?" Jeremy should be grateful I hadn't taken the elegantly carved giraffe from its spot by the entrance door and cracked it across his skull.

"He's in the bedroom. He's barely moved off the bed for the last month." I could tell by the tone of his voice, Jeremy sported a scowl.

The press had had a field day following the riot that should have been the new single launch.

Practically everywhere I looked in the ensuing weeks – whether newspapers, magazines, online forums or TV channels – the media carried images of the devastation. Young Elvis and Jeremy fronted for an "insider" fly-on-the-wall documentary crew who managed to cobble together a mishmash of lies, innuendo and old video outtakes of Jules and me to create a semi-believable piece about our crushing affair.

The end result? Jules and I had been confined to an

estate in the north of the Lake District that Dan had hastily rented under an assumed name. Nick, crippled by the shame and gossip, had a complete nervous breakdown.

A strange sense of the familiar came over me as I walked down the long hallway toward what for many years had been my bedroom. The house still smelt the same, looked the same, seemed the same. Except I knew everything to be so very different.

Sheree had called me. Jules very nearly threw my cellphone out of the window. Then he begged me not to come, and when I wouldn't concede tried to insist on coming with me.

I scotched that, knowing that if Jeremy and Jules were ever again in the same room one of them would end up in the local hospital. Instead I left Jules holed up with Otis while Verne escorted me down country. He now waited patiently in my living room with Sheree and Jeremy.

Sheree's words still echoed in my ears. "You're our last port of call."

Nick's housekeeper had found him unconscious in his car with a hose leading from the exhaust to the window. His family had never much cared for him at the best of times and now, in his time of need, due to the scandal and the suicide attempt they'd publicly abandoned him. I felt I couldn't do the same, no matter how much I loved Jules.

Jules was angry with my choice – but he wasn't suicidal.

I opened the bedroom door and was assaulted by the familiar lavender scent of my bed linen. The curtains were closed, the only light coming from a small oval reading lamp that stood at the side of the bed. Apparently he'd taken to sleeping in my room, abandoning his own.

The whole scene, Nick lying there, motionless in the half-light, reminded me of an upmarket viewing room in a funeral parlor. I shivered.

"Hi, how are you doing?" My voice sounded hoarse, even to me.

"Why would you care?" The cold monotone spoke more than the four simple words. "Who sent you?"

"Shez called. Said she couldn't get you out of bed and everyone was worried." I lingered by the door, wondering if it was inappropriate for me to be seeing a man in his bedroom, alone. Even if it did used to be my bedroom, and technically he was still my husband.

I had a sense of Jules hovering all about me. The intimacy Nick and I used to share was long gone - well and truly erased by the many nights I'd become accustomed to spending in Jules' bed.

Nonetheless, I owed the man something.

Tentatively, I stepped further into the room, navigating my way around the crushed velvet of the bedspread that pooled down one side of the king-size bed. "I see you still can't keep the bedspread off the floor."

Little more than a grunt of acknowledgement came from under the covers.

I made my way to the draped window and pulled on the weighted cord in an attempt to open the curtains and let some light in.

There had been many times during our marriage when Nick had retreated to his bedroom. Hidden in its cave-like confines until, after a few days, he emerged refreshed and able again to engage with the vagaries of life.

The drape pull jammed. Carefully I tugged down on

the opposite side of the thick cord, hoping to jiggle free the runners so the heavy material would part. Inch by inch the curtains came apart and a thin shaft of winter sunlight fell across the room, illuminating the dark.

I caught a glimpse of the hills and lake beyond the house. A view that had greeted me morning after morning in another life. The sparse light cast long golden shadows across the rolling landscape. No matter what the season, it always took my breath away. It was one of the things that had sold us on the house many years ago and, I conceded to myself miserably, one of the things I missed most about it.

"You've not hidden in here before?" I tried to sound positive.

"I've never before been publicly humiliated by my wife, had my peers judge me because she ran off with a bisexual porn star, nor had my family abandon me."

How did I answer that barrage? I remember finding him in bed when I came home from a tour. I let him stay there for four days, but then I threatened to call the doctor and have him committed. He got up then and confessed he'd been in bed for over two weeks.

I ignored his last comment and decided the practical approach was needed. "You're getting up now and you're getting dressed."

"Is that right?"

"Yes, that's right." I walked into the adjoining bathroom, and it seemed stark and bare. All my creams, my toothbrush and my toiletries missing. It looked as if I'd been erased from the area.

A single towel hung on the heated towel rail. I presumed it must be Nick's and pulled it off. I opened the clear, glass shower door and turned on the water.

"Come on. You're getting up and having a shower." It was an approach that had worked previously and I had no reason to believe it wouldn't work this time as well.

I heard a groan, and then he appeared in the small space of the bathroom. The last time we were in a bathroom together he was bleeding.

I left him alone to shower.

My stomach in a knot, I picked up my bag, which I realized I'd thrown on "my chair" in the bedroom. It was strangely alone without the mass of clothing and bric-a-brac that used to accumulate with day-to-day living whenever I came home.

Before I stepped out of the bedroom, I called out to Nick in the shower. "I need some air and to think. I'll arrange lunch for you downstairs, so make sure you're down there when I get back."

"I have a choice?" His voice, stronger now, came on the waves of steam from the shower.

"You know you don't."

"You are coming back?" The need in his voice struck me in the solar plexus.

I hesitated. "Of course I'm coming back. Why would I bother getting you out of bed if I wasn't coming back?"

Why? I wondered myself.

I made my way back down the long hallway and turned left just before the front door. I loved that door with its surrounding picture lead-lights. The colored patterns threw themselves around the white walls like a child's kaleidoscope.

Jeremy was lounging across my Italian leather lounge suite. I remembered the trip Nick and I took to purchase it. We had a massive joint history.

"He's in the shower and he'll be down shortly for the lunch I brought," I told Shez. I could scarcely look at Jeremy. Every time I did, the horror of the past few months came back to me.

"I'll make sure he eats something. I can't believe you've managed to get him out of bed." Sheree cared so much.

We went back years. It was a shame I could no longer stand to be anywhere near her husband.

"Good," Jeremy snapped. "That means you can fuck back off to that pervert you ran off with." And there, as if on cue, he gave me another reason to hate him.

I'd had enough. "If anyone's going to be doing any fucking off around here, it's you!"

The fury of the last two months took over. "You think you're God almighty - sitting there on my couch, in my house, behaving like you're some fucking saint. Well, let me tell you something, Mr Jeremy I'm-a-real-cunt-and-I-can-judge-anyone-I-feel-like. You're nothing. Just a piece of little, insignificant shit who doesn't have the courage to do a fucking single worthwhile thing with his own life."

I marched across my living room and stood over a wide-eyed Jeremy. "You've sat on your backside, living off Shez's earnings. Complaining about her being on tour. Complaining that people care about her and love her. And let me tell you, pal..." His face was going red but I didn't care anymore. "Let me tell you a few facts of life. This woman..."

I grabbed Sheree, pulled her over in front of me and presented her to Jeremy. "Let me tell you how wonderful, attractive, talented and loving this woman is. How the hell she ever got herself tied down to an insignificant, intolerable cretin like you I'll never know."

I stopped for a breath. Sheree was looking at me like I was a mad woman. Jeremy, tried to dig himself deeper into the couch, retreating from my words. Stuff it, he could have the lot.

"How long did it take you, huh? How long did it take you to track Young Elvis down? And what did you say to him? He was happy when he left us. What did you promise him? Five more minutes of fame?"

Jeremy started to look uncomfortable.

Sheree came to her senses. "Cut it out, Mags. I think you've said enough."

"I haven't said the half of it."

I turned back to Jeremy. "Was it worth it? Did you think about the effect you'd have on your good friend, Nick?" My voice rose an octave. "*Did you*?"

He started to stutter. "I...I..."

"Of course you fucking didn't. Are you happy? You've destroyed him. You've destroyed me. You've destroyed the band. Jules will never play again. I'm just hoping that you've destroyed your own life as well."

I gestured at Sheree. "You really think she's going to be happy at home, making sure the dinner's on the table for you at night? Barefoot and pregnant in the kitchen while you're out there doing your nobody job, bringing home your nobody friends and having your nobody life?"

"Mags, shut up!" Sheree screamed at me.

I yelled over her, "She might be for a couple of months. In fact, she could probably stand it for a couple of years. But you've ruined what she loves. You've taken away from her the thing in her life that's intrinsic. You've taken away from her what makes her who she is."

Jeremy went pale. "That's not true." He looked at Sheree. "It's what you want. Isn't it? Tell her."

Sheree's eyes fell to the floor. She wouldn't meet his gaze and the room fell suddenly silent.

I turned on my heel, leaving them to it.

"You fucking moron," I whispered under my breath as I stalked out the door.

Walking always made me feel better - it had ever since I could remember - and now, more than ever before, I needed soothing.

I knew Jules would be distraught but I kept my phone off. With one man having melted down and another one well on the way, the last thing I needed was Jules being a third.

I walked a familiar path beside the lake, carrying unfamiliar feelings. I wanted to be with Jules - I loved him - but I had a moral obligation to Nick. We were still married and now he had no one except me. And it was my behavior that had created the ignition for his breakdown.

It occurred to me that none of my possessions were in a storage unit at all. He'd lied to me out of anger. I only had to look at our home to see I still belonged here.

My problem. Because I didn't want to be here. But - I wrestled with myself - what choice did I have? Yes, I could run away and be with the man of my heart, but then the man I'd married would destroy himself and I would be responsible for the loss of a life. The loss of someone I had once loved and respected. But I'd never, I realized now, loved him the way I loved Jules.

The walking wasn't helping.

I stopped. Maybe sitting would help.

That was it. I needed to sit and stay still and allow the lake to work its magic.

I found myself doing something I'd not done for many years. I began to pray.

I'd allow my God to show me the way.

A coward would have told Jules over the phone. I may have been many things in my life, but a coward wasn't one of them.

I knew what I had to do. As unpalatable as the circumstances around my life had become – this was the right choice.

"Please don't make it any harder for me." I knew I sounded desperate.

Jules held me close. His arms and his scent of him surrounding me. "Why would I want to make it any easier for you?" I could hear the emotion choking up his voice and I buried my face in the warmth of his shoulder, willing myself not to cry. "You're leaving me for a man you don't even love." Pain echoed through his words and through the chambers of my heart. "How can you do this to me? How can you do this to *us*?"

"I don't want to but I have no choice." I'd wished so many times I had a choice but I could see no other way. Nick, finally out of the bedroom - and out of earshot of Sheree and Jeremy - had professed his undying love and adoration for me and told me he'd realized his life wasn't worth living without me.

"So he tried to kill himself. We'll get him a good psychiatrist. You don't have to do this." Jules was on his knees, his arms wrapped around my waist, his head tucked against my tummy.

Tears rolled down my face as I repeated my mantra. "Please, Jules, don't make this any harder." I really didn't want to, but I had to go.

CHAPTER NINETEEN

Three weeks had passed. It seemed like three months. I'd fallen back into the old familiar pattern of my life at home. The only unfamiliar thing was Nick being around all the time and the total absence of Jules from my life.

I tried to fill that aching hole, but nothing into nothing didn't work.

"Who was that?" Nick took the phone from my hand.

Dan had wanted to tell me. He said he didn't want me to hear on the news.

I turned on the TV and it was all over the entertainment channel. Jules' clothes had been found in a neatly folded pile by the lake. He was missing, presumed drowned. He hated the water - he didn't even know how to swim. What the hell had he been thinking?

I fell to my knees on the floor. Disbelief - or was it the kernels of grief I'd refused to deal with? - came together to assault me at once. Whatever, I couldn't breathe. The room began to sway at the edges.

The last thing I remember was Nick's strong arms encircling me while I wished they belonged to Jules.

* * *

I threw a stone in the lake, ripples lapped lazily at the rushes on the bank. The last time I sat here, I'd prayed. Directed by God to revisit my marriage and afraid of Nick attempting to take his life again, I made the wrong decision. I returned to Nick and left the man I loved.

My belief that Jules could move on and make a new life for himself proved to be wrong.

Now, he was lost. Not only to me, but to the thousands of others who also loved him.

Candlelight vigils were being held at the gates of his estate. Every time I saw another image of him - and they were everywhere - my heart broke again.

How could I have been so stupid? I'd betrayed the man I loved by choosing Nick and this was my punishment.

Grief settled around me and I wore it as a comfortable shroud. Just getting out of bed in the morning became an insurmountable chore. The air about me felt thick and dark, like pea soup. Life continued on around me, but my head, filled with the cotton wool of woe and uncomfortable thoughts of Jules, refused to function.

"You have to get out of bed." No matter how much Nick coaxed, nagged or threatened each day, it was always after lunchtime before I got up.

Role reversal.

"You spent weeks here. Why shouldn't I?" Resolutely I pulled the Indian cotton sheets around my shoulders and snuggled back into my comforting nest.

"Because I know you only came back to me out of a sense of duty." Nick turned on the shower. I knew there

250

was little chance of me remaining in bed for much longer. "And I won't abandon you, either. You're my wife. I'm your husband. I have a duty to ensure you are looked after."

The sheets were pulled from me and a cool draft fell across my exposed arms and legs. I never slept nude at home. I'd almost forgotten what it felt like to have a naked man's body beside me. The thought of Jules' exquisite body tortured me. I closed my eyes, trying to banish the thought, but I could see him in my mind's eye. Teasing me, taunting me.

Nick and I had tried, haltingly, to make love on a few occasions in the last months since Jules disappearance. Each fumbling effort ended in apologies and embarrassed mumblings. I might have come back to save his life, but somewhere along the way I'd lost my own and now Jules had lost his.

"It's no good trying to go back to sleep." Nick droned on at the end of the bed. This was how it had been for months and, to be fair to the memory of Jules, it had become like this long before he swam off into the night.

"I can't do this anymore, Nick."

"I know. You need to get up in the mornings and not waste half the day in bed." He had no idea what I was talking about.

"No." I swung my legs over the edge of the bed, my toes digging into the warmth of the sheepskin rug. "I mean I can't do this marriage. Be here with you."

Nick looked at me. Almost stunned. "But why would you want to leave now? He's dead!"

Nick's uncompromising grasp of logic never ceased to amaze me. It was his lack of passion and emotion I still

251

couldn't come to grips with.

"I miss him too much."

I made my way to the bathroom - a room that seemed to play a pivotal role in my life when it came to men. At the doorway I paused. "You don't need me anymore. You've got your life back over these last few months. The doctor says you're doing well. You won't even notice I'm gone."

"That's not true," he objected. "You know how much you're a part of my life."

I grasped the door, ready to close it behind me and on my stale and empty existence. "I'm a part of your life, Nick, like that chair over in the corner is a part of your life. You're used to the chair being around - it's familiar to you - but if I took that chair away it wouldn't really bother you. You might notice it had gone, but in a couple of days you'd be over it. That's how it'll be with me, Nick. You'll notice I've gone, but in a couple of days you'll be over it."

I closed the door. He knew I was right. Hell, I knew I was right.

I wished in my heart I'd come to this decision before Jules walked off on his own into the water and out of my life forever.

I took off my nightgown, stepped into the shower and allowed the hot water to wash away my bitter tears of regret.

I found a flat and looked for work. Nick, certain I'd return once I "came to my senses" paid my rent even though I had enough money put away from touring so I didn't need to work.

Riddled with grief and lamenting my loss, I threw

myself into volunteer work at the local animal shelter. I figured if I surrounded myself only with animals there would be little chance of my heart being broken ever again.

One night when I was sitting on my secondhand couch in front of the TV, dinner on my knee and a small ginger kitten - one of four I was fostering from the shelter - curled in a tight ball beside me, the phone rang. The kitten stirred slightly in its sleep, tiny outstretched claws leaving minute indentations in the fabric of the couch.

I picked up the phone. Dan's voice boomed out of the earpiece. "How's our girl?"

"I'm okay." He knew I wasn't okay, but we liked to pretend.

"I need you to come over." His voice sounded strange.

"What, tonight?"

"Yes."

"I'm tired - I've just got in from the shelter. Can't it wait?"

"No. I think you might like to hear what I have to say and you might want to hear it tonight."

"Dan, what can be so important that it can't wait until tomorrow?"

"Well..." He chuckled in a way I hadn't heard him chuckle for months. It was a sound that I remembered from touring and I had a sudden and painful thought of Jules. As much as I loved Dan, seeing him brought so much hurt. "If I told you over the phone I wouldn't get the pleasure of seeing your face."

"You're not going to let me alone, are you?"

"No. Tell you what, though, I'm feeling generous. Why don't I come to you?"

I sighed. There was just no saying no to him some days. "I guess I won't be going to bed yet, then."

"Great. You won't be sorry. I'll see you in about half an hour." He had a deep sound of satisfaction in his voice.

"Okay. Bye."

I put the phone down before he had a chance to say anything else and addressed the tiny ball of fluff on the couch. "What, I wonder, does he think he's up to now?"

"I still miss him, you know." I'd settled myself back on the couch beside the kittens, who were now tumbling over one another.

"You're not the only one." Dan looked me square in the eyes. "I miss him every day."

"I don't think I can ever forgive myself."

"You don't have to. You don't have to beat yourself up about it anymore."

"But I do."

Dan grinned at me. "You've got no idea why I'm here, have you?"

I shook my head. "No."

"Don't hate me."

"Why should I hate you?" The man was making even less sense than usual and that was saying something.

"Because I have kept something from you, but you need to know it was important that it be kept from you."

I didn't understand. "What do you mean?"

Dan paced backwards and forwards in the tiny space. "I've brought someone here to see you."

"It'd better not be fucking Shez. I never want to see her again - or that asshole husband of hers."

"Calm down. No, it's not either of them."

The door opened.

And there he was.

Should I laugh or cry?

"Jules." His name came as a whisper on my lips, as it had every night since he disappeared. Nights when I'd cried myself to sleep, my body cold and aching for his.

"How? Why? When?" I looked between the two of them, dumbstruck.

Jules covered the ground between us in an instant. I was in his arms, his lips covering mine. The urgency of his lips, his taste, his touch. Transported, my world was complete again. He consumed me and I longed to be consumed. Never again would I be without the taste, scent or touch of him. My pulse raced. I should have hated him for what he'd put me through. It took all my effort to simply breathe.

When we eventually parted I couldn't let his hand go, couldn't bear to be separated from him.

Dan, his faced flushed - from embarrassment or the pleasure of seeing us together - broke the spell of silence. "Let me introduce Mr Simon Greene."

I laughed out loud. "Simon?"

"What's wrong with Simon?" Jules kissed me on the nose, playfully.

"Nothing if you're simple," I teased.

"You mean you're not going to be happy to be Mrs Simon Greene, then?"

"You know I will."

"So are you going to tell her what happened, or shall I?" Dan interrupted.

"You've known all these months and didn't let on?" I

could have throttled him.

"He couldn't tell you. I couldn't let anyone know. I wanted to disappear and never come back."

"He's been as dead to me as he has been to you." I could tell Dan told the truth from the tone of his voice, and I knew how much he'd missed Jules over the last few months.

"How could he be dead to you and be here now?" I decided I'd definitely throttle Dan. I hated him.

"Tell her, mate." Dan grinned at Jules as if he'd been waiting for this moment for months, which he probably had been.

Jules led me by the hand, herded a couple of kittens out of the way and sat himself on the couch. He pulled me down into his lap. I began to wonder if the last nine months hadn't been some kind of awful dream. Everything seemed almost surreal.

"When you left - "

"Don't remind me." The stress of the last nine months erupted from me and I broke down into tears.

With a gentle touch he wiped them from my damp cheeks. "Shh. It's okay."

"It's not okay," I stuttered between sobs. "Everyone thinks you're dead."

"But I'm not."

"Well, technically you are," Dan interjected from the other side of the room. One of the kittens sat chewing the end of his bootlace.

Jules held his hand up, stopping Dan. "Procedural problem only."

"But how can you be here and be dead?" Panic clawed at me. "Haven't you broken the law or something?" I looked across to Dan. "Haven't you helped him? Doesn't that make you some kind of accessory to a crime?"

"What crime?" Jules' voice sounded soft and reassuring. "No one's claimed any insurance. There's been no fraud. I've simply disappeared.   Missing, presumed dead. Where's the harm in that?"

"Where's the fucking harm in that?"   Anger coursed through me, replacing sorrow in the same way the first heat-wave of summer thaws the cool autumn ground. "I'll tell you where the fucking harm is..." I started punching him in the chest. Hard.

"Steady on." He gripped my thin wrists, holding them tight against his battered torso.

"The harm is that you broke my heart. I thought you were dead."

"You left me - for him. Remember? I think we might be even."

"How could I ever forget! But then you let me believe you were dead. If I didn't love you so much I'd kill you with my bare hands."

He pulled my face to his. His lips slanted over mine. My mouth opened, allowing his probing tongue to take me. If Dan hadn't been in the room I'd have allowed him to take me completely where we sat.

Embarrassed, I broke away. Jules simply smiled at me.

"We can always send young Dan home and carry on this discussion." He grinned, a gleam in his green eyes - eyes I'd longed to see for so many months.

"You've got the rest of your lives for that." Dan cut into the conversation.   "Get on with telling the poor woman what happened."

"Yeah."   My composure began to return in small

257

increments. "Tell me why it's not a good idea for me to kill you and just dispose of your body now. No one's going to miss you." I winked at Dan. "It would be the perfect crime."

Jules tickled me then.

"Oy! Quit it and get on with your story."

"Okay." He wriggled under me, settling me more comfortably into his lap. "Where was I?"

"When she left..." Dan decided to give him a helping hand.

"Ah, yes." Jules looked me in the eyes again. "When you left me, my world fell apart. I realized you were the rock my entire empire had been built on. Without you I couldn't survive. I didn't care the band was over, that my reputation had been ruined, or that I'd never tour again."

"I said you could work and tour again, but you wouldn't listen to me." Dan had cut in again.

"And I told you I didn't want to tour again. I'd promised this beautiful lady here we'd make a life together and I meant it."

"But-" I glanced over at Dan "-when I left he could have worked again."

Dan shrugged. "I agree with you. That's what I told him but he wouldn't."

I asked Jules, "Why didn't you go back to work?"

He began to draw small circles on one leg of my faded blue jeans. "I hoped you'd eventually tire of him and come back to me."

"But I didn't."

"No, you didn't. So I decided after nearly four months that the only thing I could do was vanish. It was going to be hard to just go somewhere. You know what it's like -

everyone's always looking for me."

"You get no peace." I remembered.

"So I decided I'd just have to die and then I could be alone. Go and live someplace new - near a beach I decided, somewhere I'd have liked to live with you."

"So you faked your death and the brother Grimm over there helped you."

Dan grinned at me from across the room.

"I should throttle you as well. How could you put me through the last five months?"

"Jules needed to disappear and...well, quite frankly we thought about getting him back pretty quick.. You know, after you left Nick. But we needed to be sure you weren't going to go back to him again."

I narrowed my eyes and I had to admit, I could see their point. "So. What now, chaps?"

Jules kissed me again. Long and hard, with a hunger that spoke of months of yearning. "Do you still love me?"

"I do." With more passion than I would ever understand.

"Will you abandon everything you know and come with me to the other side of the world? Live a simple life by the beach and bear my children?"

"I will, on a couple of conditions."

Jules cocked his head. "And they would be."

"That you promise me you'll contribute to this simple life you want. I'm not waiting on you hand and foot. You'll do your share."

He didn't hesitate. "Done. And what's your second condition?"

"You tell me you love me every day."

"That's a no-brainer."

"I guess it's settled then." Dan cut in. "I'll make sure we have those plane tickets booked by the end of the week." He threw me a wink. "In the meantime I'm going to go home and leave you two lovebirds to get reacquainted. There's groceries in the hallway to keep you fed. I don't want either of you leaving the flat. I'll see myself out."

As the front door shut behind Dan, Jules picked me up and spun me round. "I guess you'd better show me to your bedroom." His smile lit his face. "You won't regret this."

I grinned back at him. "I know."

"You won't leave me?" A flash of uncertainty crossed his face.

"Never. Never again. Not till death parts us." And I knew this to be the truth.

My truth.

His truth.

Our eternal truth.

You've finished!

If you enjoyed Mags and Julian's story please take a moment to write a short review and rate the book on your favorite review site.

Book 2 of the **PRIVATE LOVE** series is underway.

In the meantime, you might want to get to know Matt

and Tamsen - CATCH is available now:

Tamsen Parsons is happy with her wacky world. So she leases fish to big business, her bedroom resembles a gypsy fortune-teller's caravan and she's got the flat-mate from hell. Still, the sun's shining and she can smile.

That is until uptight lawyer Matthew Solomon breaks into her serene world. He's over the corporate climb, unsure what he wants in life anymore and the sexy and aloof Tamsen looks like just the sort of short-term tonic he needs.

What Matt doesn't count on is his interfering mother, Tamsen's out-of-control best friend and falling in love.

Can a gypsy-fish-minder really bring this bad-boy to heel?

A Personal Message from Toni Kenyon:

I love writing books! But even more than that I love hearing from my readers. If you've enjoyed this book, or any other of my books, please take a moment to email me and introduce yourself - I always respond personally to my readers.

I would also love to put you on my mailing list to receive notifications about future books, updates and contests. I promise you won't be inundated!

Please visit http://www.tonikenyon.com/contact and introduce yourself so I can personally thank you for trying my books or follow me on Facebook - I'll hear from you soon.

Romance from Toni Kenyon - a fresh look at the world

Acknowledgments

There's always a lot of people to thank when you publish a first book - these are just a few of the wonderful people in my life who support me and my artistic endeavors:

Mum, for encouraging me to read and giving me the gritty determination needed to see this through to the last word. I love you.

Dad, for instilling in me a love of music. I wish you were here.

Mark, for insisting that I turn on the computer every night, make a cup of tea and 'just write'. You're wise beyond your years my darling boy - you always have been.

Phil, for understanding that Mum needed to play with the people who talked in her head - and for scoring the family 'music' gene - don't let anyone talk you out of your dreams!

Kevin, for always believing in me. For understanding my burning desire to create and encouraging me every day to take one small step toward my destiny. A great love.

Thank you, Andrew for teaching me about the process of creating music, for sharing your stories about life in the industry and on the road and for not whining when I wasn't available for vocal sessions.

I couldn't have done this without Romance Writers of New Zealand and the BILDers - I love you girls.

BILDers Rock!